pirouette

# pirouette

ROBYN BAVATI

flux
™
Woodbury, Minnesota

First Edition
First Printing, 2013

Book design by Bob Gaul
Cover design by Ellen Lawson
Cover image: iStockphoto.com/19855750/enderstse, 22148063/AnnaPaff
          SuperStock.com/1598R-125025/Exactostock

Flux, an imprint of Llewellyn Worldwide Ltd.

**Library of Congress Cataloging-in-Publication Data**
Bavati, Robyn.
  Pirouette/Robyn Bavati.—First edition.
      pages cm
  Summary: "When Simone and Hannah, fifteen-year-old identical twins, meet for the first time at dance camp, they switch places in order to change the role that dance plays in their lives"—Provided by publisher.
  ISBN 978-0-7387-3481-1
  [1. Dance—Fiction. 2. Twins—Fiction. 3. Sisters—Fiction. 4. Mistaken identity—Fiction. 5. Orphans—Fiction.] I. Title.
  PZ7.B3287Pi 2013
  [Fic]—dc23

                                        2013010463

Flux
Llewellyn Worldwide Ltd.
2143 Wooddale Drive
Woodbury, MN 55125-2989
www.fluxnow.com

Printed in the United States of America

For Mum, who is also a Gemini

# prologue

The young nurse was hurrying to the kitchen when she heard a cry. It was time to heat the bottles for the afternoon feed, but, unable to bear the thought of leaving a baby in distress, she headed back to the nursery that housed the youngest infants.

Apart from the odd snuffle, whimper, or sigh, it was fairly quiet. She peeped into one crib after another, tucking in blankets, gently stroking those who were fretting. She wished she could give each and every one of these babies more of her time, but there were so many children to take care of, and the orphanage was woefully understaffed.

She was about to head back to the kitchen when her eye fell upon the corner crib and she couldn't resist a peek inside. This crib was slightly larger than the others, for in it lay not one infant, but two—two little girls who were simply exquisite, and absolutely identical.

Marcela loved all the children in her care, but none so much as these special two. Their parents had died as a result of a freak accident on the way to the hospital, just as the car was approaching the hospital grounds. The babies' father was killed outright; their mother hung on a few minutes more, allowing the hospital staff to deliver the girls by Caesarean section.

Now, oblivious to the events surrounding their birth, the four-week-old twins lay on their backs, side by side, one with a tiny fist clasped tight around the other's finger. Soft, cooing sounds issued from their delicate throats, as if they were having a conversation.

Marcela smiled as she watched them, but her smile faded as her gaze moved to the recently updated charts clipped onto the crib.

Every infant had a chart, and every chart listed important information about the child: date of birth, current weight and birth weight, mother's name if known. It also listed basic details about the child's adoptive parents, and it was this information that caused the nurse's brow to crease in concern.

For while one twin was to be adopted by a single woman in Melbourne, Australia, the other seemed destined to become part of a family in Houston, Texas.

Marcela's heart went out to the unsuspecting baby girls. It would be wrong for them to lose each other; it was bad enough that they had lost their parents.

———

Though not unexpected, it was a shock when Marcela came to work one morning to find only a single infant in the corner crib. The night nurse reported that the baby girl had howled for most of the night; indeed, tears were still drying on her sad little face.

Marcela had coaxed and pleaded with Beatriz, the woman in charge of the orphanage, to reconsider, but Beatriz had said the decision was not hers to make.

"Twins are meant to be kept together," Marcela protested. "It's government policy."

"Yes, Marcela, just like it's government policy that babies born in Brazil should be adopted by Brazilian families. But private adoption agencies are not always bound by government policy. There are not enough Brazilian families with the means to adopt, and there are so many childless families overseas. Perhaps the agency feels it's unfair to give two babies to one family and none to another."

"But if the parents *knew* there were two, then maybe they'd—"

"*Basta,* Marcela! Both the babies will be loved and cared for. It is out of my hands."

Now, as Marcela began the morning shift, she plied the night nurse for information. "Did you see the Australian woman?"

The night nurse nodded. "She wanted to know all about the baby's parents."

"What did you tell her?"

"Beyond the circumstances of the parents' death? Only that the child's mother was a ballet dancer who came to Brazil with the Paris Opera and remained here when she fell in love with a Brazilian boy."

"You didn't mention the baby's sister?"

"How could I, Marcela? I'd lose my job." The night nurse yawned and rubbed her eyes.

"But—"

"*Bom dia*, Marcela. I'm going home now. I really must sleep."

After the night nurse left, Marcela gave all the babies their weekly weigh-in and entered the current figures on their charts. Very few, she saw, were destined to remain in their country of birth. One little boy would soon be on his way to England, one to Greece, another to Israel. And one sweet little girl had been promised to a couple in … Marcela's breath caught in her throat and she read the name of the place again, just to be sure.

Yes, there was no doubt about it—the little girl was scheduled to leave for Melbourne, Australia. In fact, the couple were coming to collect her the very next day.

Unbelievable though it seemed, this child had the same birth date as the twins, and was a similar weight. Like them, her skin was the color of light caramel, and the soft, silky down that covered her head was just a shade darker than theirs.

Making sure she was unobserved, Marcela scooped the baby into her arms, carried her gently to the corner crib, and placed her inside. Then she picked up the remaining twin, who was sound asleep.

"*Não preocupes tu,*" Marcela whispered. "Don't worry, little baby. You too will travel to Melbourne, Australia." She kissed the infant's forehead, gently so as not to wake her, and laid her carefully in the empty crib.

Then she went back to work, for she'd done all she could.

Now, only Fate would determine the future of the baby twins. But at least she'd given Fate a push in the right direction...

*Fifteen years and
five months later*

# one

Simone Stark flung open the door to the nearest cubicle and dropped to her knees, head poised over the toilet bowl. Afraid she'd throw up again, she tried to focus on her breathing —in for two counts, out for four—but it was hard to get an even rhythm when her whole body was trembling.

The bathroom door crashed open and Simone held her breath.

"Simone! Are you in here?" That was Jess, Simone's best friend.

Simone heaved herself up and opened the stall door.

Jess was already in costume and fully made up. "You missed your call," she said. "Mr. Dixon is fuming. Hey, are you okay?"

Simone shook her head as she crept toward the bathroom sink, catching sight of her own reflection—face flushed, eyes bloodshot and puffy, strands of lank, untidy hair plastered to her sweating forehead.

"I'll tell Miss Sabto."

"No." Simone turned on the tap and scooped handfuls of water into her mouth and over her eyes. "It's too late for me to back out now."

"But—"

"My mum will freak out if she doesn't see me on that stage. How long have I got?"

"About twenty-five minutes."

"I can't go into the dressing room like this. Can you bring me my costume and makeup?"

Jess looked doubtful.

"Please, Jess."

"Yeah, okay."

———

Fifteen minutes later, Simone looked every bit the calm and elegant ballerina in her golden tutu and flesh-colored tights. Her makeup was heavily and artfully applied, and artificial flowers were threaded through hair that was slicked back tightly into a bun.

Eyeing the stranger in the mirror, Simone wondered at the irony of it—the great chasm between who she really was and who she seemed.

"There," said Jess, giving Simone's hair one final spray.

They hurried backstage, where dancers were flexing and stretching their muscles to keep them warm.

Luckily, Mr. Dixon was nowhere in sight, but Miss Sabto was frantic. "Simone, I'd just about given up on you. Where on earth have you been?"

"I had an upset stomach."

"Hmm! Probably nerves. Don't worry. They'll fall away the moment you step onstage."

*Wrong*, thought Simone. That used to happen. Not anymore.

If only she didn't have to perform today—or any day. If only she could make it all go away. But the orchestra had started playing to a packed and eager audience, and she was on any minute with a classical solo.

"Knock 'em dead," said Jess.

Sick with dread, but smiling out into the darkened theater as she'd been trained, Simone slowly revealed one pointed foot after another as she made her entrance, trying to comfort herself with the thought that the show would soon be over.

She had four dances to get through—ballet, contemporary, jazz, and tap—and each performance was just as stressful as the one before.

When she took her final bows, the applause rolled over her. Her head ached and she wished the audience would stop making such a racket. She wanted to lie down and close her eyes. She wanted to snap her fingers and find herself in bed, asleep. She wanted to sleep for a long, long time.

At last, the curtain came down and the ordeal was over. It would be months before she had to go through it again.

On the car ride home, Harriet Stark kept up a running critique of the evening's performance—and all the dancers. "You were the best, of course," she told her daughter. "Matthew Holden's turned into a fine young dancer. Jess wasn't bad. Didn't think much of Alison Boyd—I honestly don't know how that girl got into the school."

Simone stared out the window, trying to block out the sound of her mother's voice. She wished she had the strength to tell her not to be so harsh and judgmental, but she was too tired to speak.

———

The digital clock read 12:05. It was the first day of the summer holidays. For the first time in months, Simone had been able to sleep as late as she liked. Still, she woke feeling numb and out of sorts. She lay in bed a while longer, her limbs heavy from sleep. It wasn't until she tried to move that she became aware of her aching muscles. The dull pain brought back the memory of the night before, and the months of hard work leading up to it. Thank God the year had finally ended, and she'd have six whole weeks without a single dance class.

She got up and made her way slowly into the kitchen. Harriet was out and Simone was alone. She poured herself a glass of juice and sat down to drink it. It was only then that her eye fell upon the cream-colored envelope at the edge of the table, and her heart sank at the sight of the familiar letterhead.

The envelope was addressed to her. She tore it open and skimmed it briefly.

*Dear Simone,*

*We are pleased to confirm your place at Candance…*
*Enclosed, please find your receipt for…*
*Should you have any special requests or requirements,*
*don't hesitate to…*

Simone felt anger rise within her. Had her mother really booked her into Candance again when she'd specifically said she did not want to go?

It was bad enough attending the VSD—the Victorian School of Dance—during the year, where full-time dance training was combined with regular academic studies. But the thought of full-time dancing in the holidays was just too much to bear.

Curbing a sudden urge to shred the letter into tiny pieces, Simone opened her hand and watched it fall. It landed face-up on the table, and she stared at it until her vision blurred and the black print swam before her eyes.

Harriet came home an hour later. "What is it, Simone?"

"You booked me into Candance." Simone was on the verge of tears. "I told you I didn't want to go."

Harriet kept her voice light as she said, "What's so terrible about Candance?"

"I'm supposed to be on holiday. I need a break."

"Of course you do," said Harriet, "and you'll have one. Candance doesn't start for another three weeks."

"*I don't want to go.*"

"Nonsense, Simone. You always enjoy it. And it'll give you an advantage over the other students when you start Year Ten. Besides, it's been booked and paid for."

# two

As she stood in the wings, heart pounding, pulse racing, Hannah Segal felt as if she might explode. The final minutes before a performance were always sheer agony, and tonight was no exception. The younger students were always on first, so Hannah had been waiting for over half an hour. She wished she could fast-forward time.

Then wonderfully, magically, the music for her dance began, and finally she burst onto the stage and into the spotlight.

Nothing was quite as exhilarating as dancing in front of a large audience—at no other time did she feel so intensely alive. As she leaped across the stage in her sleeveless red and yellow unitard, she looked like a streak of fire or a bolt of lightning.

In a flash, the dance was over, and Hannah left the stage to a roar of applause.

After three more dances—each as dreamlike and wonderful as the one before—Hannah found herself taking her final bows along with the rest of the students from her dance school. Minutes later, after changing back into her street clothes, she floated through a sea of people in the foyer.

Straight away she spotted her dad, who towered over everyone else.

"Hannah, my love! What a tremendous performance," he said as he embraced her.

"You were wonderful, darling," said her mother, kissing her cheek.

"That was cool, sis," said thirteen-year-old Adam, her younger brother.

Within seconds, Hannah was surrounded by more relatives, along with several friends from Carmel College.

"Way to go, Hannah," called her best friend Dani, pushing a path toward her through the noisy crowd.

Hannah couldn't stop grinning.

The only feeling that could equal dancing onstage was the buzz that came after—all the excitement and none of the tension.

If only it could last forever!

———

Hannah woke up smiling, remembering the night before.

She loved performing, loved that sense of losing herself inside the dance and bringing pleasure to an audience who'd become so engrossed in what was happening onstage that, for a while at least, they forgot their problems.

She lay in bed, relaxed and happy, recalling the almost

unbearable excitement that preceded the show, the concentration of energy that enabled her to perform at her very best, and the warmth of applause.

She wished she could repeat the whole experience sometime soon...

But Armadale Dance was just a local dance school. She'd have to wait an entire year for the next annual production.

Hannah felt something sink inside her. She didn't want to wait so long. Nor did she want to face the prospect of a whole summer without a single dance class.

If only she were able to attend Candance—the famous summer intensive. For years she'd wanted to fly to Canberra for the popular summer school, but every year her parents had said she was too young to spend three weeks alone. This year, she'd finally convinced them that at fifteen and a half she was old enough, but by the time they'd agreed, there were no places left. Though her name had been put on a waiting list, she didn't hold out much hope of being able to go.

Hannah sighed. She loved her parents. They were warm, wonderful people, and she often thought of herself as having won the lottery. But Manfred and Vanessa Segal had one failing —they'd never really understood her need to dance. That was the real reason they hadn't allowed her to go to Candance the previous year, or the year before that. The truth was, they thought that too much dancing would interfere with her education, and though they let her dance three times a week, they didn't want her "getting unrealistic ideas about becoming a dancer."

Hannah climbed out of bed feeling downhearted. Just

moments before, the day had seemed so full of promise. Now, despite—or perhaps because of—the thrill of the night before, she felt oddly flat. The six-week vacation loomed ahead of her—long and empty.

A knock on the door interrupted her thoughts.

"Hannah, sweetie, I've made you pancakes. You must be hungry."

"Thanks, Mum." Hannah opened the door, and the smell of something sweet and doughy lured her downstairs.

She was swallowing her last mouthful when the phone rang.

"Could you get that?" called Vanessa, who was just leaving for Malvern Medical Center, where she worked as a GP four days a week.

Hannah picked up the phone absentmindedly, thinking it might be Dani or one of her other friends from Carmel College.

The voice on the line was unfamiliar. "Could I speak to Hannah Segal?"

"Speaking," said Hannah.

"This is Jocelyn Jones from Candance Summer School. I'm calling to let you know that we've had a cancellation. You're next on the waiting list, so if you'd like to join us at Candance—"

"I would," said Hannah, before the woman could finish the sentence.

# three

The automatic doors opened as Simone approached Domestic Departures. She entered the cool interior of the terminal, then stopped abruptly. For a second, she thought she saw a girl who looked exactly like her—the same long chestnut hair, the same warm complexion, the same green eyes...

Simone blinked and looked again, but the girl had gone.

A few steps ahead, Harriet stopped when she realized her daughter wasn't beside her. "Simone, what's wrong?"

Simone barely heard. She was scanning the faces of the people around her, hoping to spot the girl again, but she was nowhere in sight. How had she disappeared so quickly? Perhaps she'd gone back inside the terminal...

Simone turned back for one last look through the automatic doors. They were glass, and so shiny they were almost invisible. *Like mirrors*, she thought. Of course! That was it. She must have seen her own reflection. In which case, she and the other girl would have been dressed identically. Had they been? She couldn't remember; it had all happened so quickly.

"Hurry up, Simone. You'll miss your plane."

Simone wished she had the courage to refuse to go.

———————

As the plane flew higher in the sky and Melbourne grew smaller before her eyes, Simone became more and more miserable. Now it really was too late to turn back. She leaned back in her seat and closed her eyes. The three-week break from dancing had done little to alleviate her exhaustion, and all she really wanted to do with her summer was relax. Now there was no chance of that. Once again she was on her way to Candance, where she'd have a busy schedule of ballet, jazz, and contemporary dance.

Simone let out a heavy sigh. She knew that everything her mother did was with her interests at heart, and she hated the thought of appearing ungrateful. But she felt crushed under the weight of her mother's ambition.

The worst thing about being adopted, Simone thought as the stewardess handed her a glass of juice, was that you felt so indebted—though perhaps children raised by their biological parents felt just as beholden and just as reluctant to upset them.

The plane rocked unsteadily as it hit a patch of turbulence, and the *Fasten Seat Belt* sign flashed on. For a second Simone thought she might throw up. She was reminded of the last time she *had* thrown up—less than half an hour before her last performance, three weeks earlier. She'd barely made it to the stage on time.

At one time, Simone had loved performing, had loved the limelight. But since starting at the VSD three years ago, she'd come to dread it. Instead of feeling more at home onstage as she'd grown older, she'd become increasingly tense and nervous with each performance—a fact that no one seemed to notice, as she'd learned to hide it. The worst of it was that it was ruining her love of dance. Once she had loved ballet with a passion; now she was starting to hate it.

*If we crash*, she thought as the plane lurched sideways, *and I die on the spot, all my problems will be solved*. Alarmed that such a drastic thought had even entered her head, Simone vowed to talk to her mother just as soon as she was back in Melbourne. Her mum just had to know that she couldn't continue living the life that was planned for her, no matter how disappointing that might be.

But first, she had three weeks of dance to contend with.

———

Hannah fled the airport, biting back tears. Now she would miss the first, the most important, day of Candance, and there wasn't a thing she could do about it. The plane she was scheduled to fly out on had developed engine trouble, and though there were two more flights to Canberra that day, both were full, and she'd been informed at the check-in that even if there were any last-minute cancellations, priority would be given to those passengers who had arrived before her and were already on stand-by. She would just have to come back again the following day.

As Hannah waited stoically for the bus that would take her back to the city, a part of her wanted to commiserate with family or friends. Her phone was in her bag, but she didn't trust herself to use it, suspecting that at the first sound of a friendly voice, the tears she was struggling to keep at bay would finally burst into full-blown sobs.

Besides, who would she call? Her mum would be busy at the clinic, her phone switched off. There was always her dad, who'd driven her to the airport earlier and wanted to wait till she'd boarded the plane, but Hannah had insisted he leave. If she called him now, he'd drop whatever he was doing and rush straight back. But right now she wasn't sure she wanted to be around his good-natured effusiveness.

She needed time to nurse her disappointment on her own.

Only half an hour earlier, she'd been so excited, so full of enthusiasm. Everything around her had looked rich and vibrant. Now the world seemed drab and leached of color.

She was still trying not to cry as the bus pulled up and she hoisted her suitcase into the baggage compartment. But her eyes were watery and her vision blurred as she climbed on board and took a seat toward the back. She couldn't remember ever feeling quite so frustrated.

As the bus made its way along the City Link, Hannah stared out the window, unseeing. It seemed absurd that she was heading away from the airport, when all she wanted to do was board that plane.

———

Except for Kimmy, the Segals' faithful hound, the house was deserted when Hannah came home. The Labrador, as always sensing when something was wrong, rubbed against her, his mournful-dog eyes oozing compassion. Hannah knelt down beside him and buried her face in his golden fur, her damp eyes turning it a muddy brown.

By the time Vanessa came home from work, Hannah was standing in the kitchen quietly gazing out of the window. Out of the corner of her eye, she saw her mother give a little jump.

"Hannah! What are you doing here? I thought I'd seen a ghost. You should have been in Canberra hours ago."

Dry-eyed now but still subdued, Hannah struggled to maintain her composure. "The flight was cancelled. They said I have to go back tomorrow."

"Oh, sweetie!" Vanessa threw her arms around her daughter. "Are you sure you can't get on a plane tonight?"

Hannah shook her head, her voice breaking as she answered. "They said that all the flights are full. There's a shortage of planes."

The kindness in her mother's face almost made Hannah start weeping all over again, but she pulled herself together when Adam sauntered in. His iPod peeped out of one pocket and he was singing along to "What's Eatin' You." Hannah grimaced. More ironic than the song's name was the fact that it was by a band called Airborne.

Noticing his sister, Adam stopped mid-song. "Hey, I thought you'd gone."

"Nope." She tried to turn it into a joke. "You're stuck with me for one more night."

"Cool," said Adam.

Hannah followed him into the living room. Hanging out with her brother had to be better than moping in her room. But as she sat beside him on the couch, staring at the large TV, she had no idea what was on the screen.

Manfred walked in just as the show was finishing. Having clearly been briefed by Vanessa, he showed no sign of surprise. "Hannah, my love! I can't tell you how happy it makes me to have you with us another day. I was missing you already." He leaned down to kiss her.

Hannah pulled a face at him and pretended to stick her fingers down her throat. Deep down, though, she was glad she had such loving parents. It was good to be wanted.

Later that night, as she lay in bed, she forced herself to look on the bright side. Tomorrow, come what may, she'd be on that plane.

She conjured up an image of a bright, airy studio, a group of passionate students and even more passionate teachers. She saw herself perfecting every step.

Finally, listening to "My Love" on her iPod and thinking of a moving contemporary performance she'd seen on *So You Think You Can Dance*, she fell asleep to visions of herself as the female dancer, flinging herself headlong into the powerful arms of her love-struck partner.

# four

"I forgot to give you this," said Manfred the following morning, slipping his Kindle into his daughter's overnight bag. "I've downloaded a few more new releases."

Hannah looked up from her bowl of cornflakes. "Dad, I don't think I'll have time to read."

"Sure you will. At least on the plane." He picked up Hannah's bright red suitcase and carried it out to the trunk of the car, while Vanessa once again issued last-minute instructions, as if in the space of twenty-four hours Hannah might have forgotten them. "Now, remember to call me as soon as you arrive."

"I will, Mum."

"And if you've forgotten anything, just go buy it."

"Yes, Mum."

"Have you got your bankcard and your credit card?"

"Uh-huh."

"I guess you're all set then. Oh, just one more thing. If you get homesick—"

"I won't."

"Okay," said Vanessa, planting a kiss on her daughter's cheek. "Fingers crossed that everything goes smoothly at the airport this time. And I hope you have a really wonderful time."

"Thanks, Mum."

"I'll miss you."

"It's only three weeks." Hannah bent down and put her arms around Kimmy's neck, allowing him to lick her face. "Don't worry," she said. "It's not like I'll be gone forever."

Adam, just in from a morning swim at the neighbor's pool, came pushing past them. "Are you still here?" Barefoot and wearing a pair of board shorts, he reeked of chlorine.

"Can't wait to get rid of me, huh?" It was meant as a joke, but there was an unexpected tightening in her chest as Hannah hugged her brother goodbye.

———————

Simone woke up with the sun streaming in through the window. Though the curtains were drawn, they didn't quite meet in the middle, and in any case they were too thin to keep the room in darkness. The bed opposite hers was empty. Everyone else in the dorm had a roommate, but for some reason Simone's roommate hadn't arrived. Though there were advantages to having a room to herself, like she did at home, it did feel lonely.

Simone brushed her teeth, showered, put on a leotard

and tights, and slipped a skirt on top. Then she left the dorm and headed over to the Caff for breakfast.

Chatting eagerly among themselves, the other dance students were all looking forward to the day ahead: meeting the teachers, finding out what repertoires and routines they'd be performing in three weeks' time, and most of all, doing what they liked best—dancing. Simone couldn't help feeling like an outsider as snippets of their conversation reached her. The others all seemed so thrilled to be there. She alone wished she were elsewhere.

She thought of her mother, who'd already rung to ask her whether she'd been placed in the correct level—the highest one—and who her teachers were. Harriet would expect a full report, no details spared. Simone sighed.

She looked at the variety of breakfast foods her fellow students were tucking into. Though she had no appetite, she knew she'd need energy to get through the day. *I must stop feeling sorry for myself,* she thought. She forced herself to swallow a mouthful of toast, then made her way over to the studio for the compulsory warm-up.

Several of the other dancers had arrived before her. Some were stretching, while others were chatting, making introductions or catching up with friends they hadn't seen in nearly a year.

Simone looked around to see if she recognized anyone from previous summers. A boy with a pale face and sandy hair looked familiar, but she couldn't quite place him. Then she remembered—he lived in Canberra, and his name was Liam. He'd been a little on the short side last time she'd seen him, but he'd grown in the past eleven months. Now he towered over the rest of the class.

Next to him was a guy Simone had never met, with dark wavy hair and large brown eyes. He had classic, sculpted features, and Simone found herself staring. He must have felt her eyes on his face, because suddenly he turned and looked straight at her. Simone blushed and looked away.

"Hey, Simone!" A striking girl with long, long legs and coal-black hair was calling her name. This was Sam, her friend from Sydney who came to Candance every year. They gave each other an affectionate hug. "How are you?" Sam started doing warm-up prances as she spoke and rushed on without waiting for an answer. "We've got Virginia Roth for warm-up and ballet. I'm so psyched I can't wait to start."

"Looks like you don't have to," said Simone as the famed Miss Roth appeared in the doorway.

"Great to see you all," the ex-principal dancer said with a smile. "I'll just do a quick roll call before we begin. We'll start with the boys. Mitchell Brock?"

"Here."

"Liam Cousins?"

"Yeah."

"Tom Delaney?"

"That's me," said the new guy, looking directly at Simone. She bit her lip and looked away, making a mental note to keep her eyes on the teacher for the rest of the lesson.

# five

"I think I should wait," said Manfred. "What if they send you home again?"

"They won't, Dad. What are the odds?"

"Even so," Manfred said, "I'd rather wait till you board the plane."

"Dad, please. I'll be okay. And Mum said you've got a meeting." Hannah flung her arms around her father's neck, then stepped away. "Go on. I'll be fine." But a moment later she was enfolded in one of his trademark bear hugs.

"Bye, Dad." This time she gave him a firm push in the direction of the car park, and twenty minutes later, she was on the plane.

Finally, the disappointment of the delayed departure was behind her and all her natural exuberance returned. It was all she could do to stop herself from bouncing up and down in her seat as she watched the suburbs of Melbourne grow smaller and more distant.

It took just over an hour to reach Canberra, and it was

a little after one o'clock when the taxi drew up to a building on a university campus. The words *School of Dance* were engraved in black and gold lettering on the pale brick wall, and a brightly colored banner was strung across the entrance. On it, in a large, decorative print, were the words *Welcome to Candance Summer School.*

As Hannah entered the building, dancers poured out of the open doorways, heading outside. Having left air-conditioned studios for the warm outdoors, they reached for their water bottles. It was certainly hotter in Canberra than it had been in Melbourne.

Ignoring a small pang of misgiving at the thought of having missed a precious morning session, Hannah looked for the office; she still had to register. It was down the other end of the corridor, and as she made her way toward it, she passed one empty studio after another.

In one studio, though, the last of the morning classes was still in progress. Hannah stopped and peered in through the window. Three or four boys were executing a series of *grand jetés en tournant* in a large circle around the room, their jumps bold and impressive. The girls were taking turns running into the center of the circle and practicing their *fouettés*.

Hannah watched, enthralled. *Fouettés en tournant* were so hard to master that it was generally only the prima ballerina who performed them onstage. They were often considered the measure of a dancer's technique, since it took precision, strength, and stamina to keep on spinning while remaining centered.

Hannah glanced at the schedule posted by the door,

not at all surprised to discover that this class was Advanced Plus, the highest level. She was enrolled in Advanced, and even that, she expected, would be quite a challenge.

Torn between wanting to stay and watch and knowing that she should really go and register, Hannah was about to move on when her attention was arrested by the girl who'd just taken up the center position. As she launched into a succession of thirty-two *fouettés*, it became obvious right away that this girl was an incredibly well-trained dancer. But it wasn't just her perfect balance and exquisite technique that kept Hannah rooted to the spot. It was the girl herself.

She had the same build as Hannah, the same tawny hair and light olive complexion. It was almost as if Hannah were watching herself—not that she was anywhere near as accomplished. Yet this girl didn't seem especially pleased or proud of her achievement. On the contrary, she just seemed glad when it was over. Now she was saying something to the teacher, and the teacher was nodding, and a moment later the girl was moving in Hannah's direction.

Hannah stepped away from the door as the girl opened it, and then they were standing face to face, staring at each other, open-mouthed.

"Wow, you're…" Hannah began, and then she was lost for words.

"Simone," said the girl. "I'm Simone."

"I'm Hannah."

———

At first Simone was silent as the two girls continued to stare at each other.

"You were at the airport yesterday," she said at last.

Hannah looked surprised.

"It was you, wasn't it?" Simone persisted.

Hannah nodded.

"I thought … that I might have imagined it."

Hannah smiled. "It is pretty amazing, isn't it?" Her voice sounded just like a recording of Simone's.

"Yeah. They say that everyone has a double, but … wow! We even sound alike."

"We do," said Hannah. "And we have the same build. But you're a much better dancer."

Simone shrugged. "I dance full-time."

"Lucky you!"

The corridor had emptied out and Simone glanced through the studio window. Her class was winding up, the dancers taking their bows and curtsies.

"We need to talk about … this," she said, waving her hand between herself and Hannah. "Before the others come out."

"Somewhere private," Hannah added.

Simone nodded. "We can talk in my room."

Hannah hesitated. "I'm supposed to go and register. I was on my way to the office when I saw you dancing. I've just arrived."

"But I've only got an hour before my next class. You can register later. The office will be open till seven o'clock."

"But—"

"Pl*eeea*se?" begged Simone.

"I don't want to miss the afternoon classes," Hannah began.

Simone sighed. "Sorry to be the one to break it to you, but you won't be able to dance today. You missed warm-up class this morning, and they're really strict about it. No warm-up, no dancing."

"But—"

"Don't look so disappointed," said Simone. "I'm dying to find out more about you."

"Yeah, okay."

"Great! Can you give me a second?" Simone dashed into the girls' changing room and slipped her feet into a pair of scuffs. She wound a wrap-around skirt around her waist and hurried back out, shoving her pointe shoes into a bag. "Come on, let's go."

Outside, groups of students having lunch together dotted the lawn. They were too engrossed in conversation to pay much attention to the identical girls, and too far away to see the resemblance between them.

"It's lucky no one's close enough to notice," said Simone. "I don't think I'm ready to answer any awkward questions."

"No," said Hannah. "Neither am I."

Simone led the way across the grass, toward the dorm, while Hannah followed, wheeling her suitcase behind her.

# SIX

Hannah put her suitcase down and looked around. The room was clean but fairly basic. There were two beds—one made up, the other bare—and a large window overlooking the extensive grounds. There was a large built-in wardrobe, and a door just inside the entrance that opened onto a small bathroom.

"I'm supposed to have a roommate," Simone said as Hannah eyed the unoccupied bed," but she hasn't turned up yet."

Hannah threw her a questioning look.

"Everyone else arrived yesterday," Simone explained, "except the girl who was meant to room with me."

"*I* was meant to arrive yesterday," Hannah said, grinning.

The two girls giggled, and for an awkward moment, neither one knew what to say.

Hannah was the first to break the silence. "It couldn't just be a coincidence, could it, that you look like me?"

Simone didn't answer right away. She was busy studying Hannah's features.

"Let's go look in the mirror," she said at last, "and see just how alike we really are." Hannah followed her into the bathroom and they stood side by side, gazing at themselves and each other in the mirror.

Despite their different hairstyles, their similarity was undeniable. Simone took the pins out of her bun, removed the hair net, and allowed her hair to fall. She brushed it out, then handed the brush to Hannah, who gave her own hair a few deft strokes. Simone's hair was about six centimeters longer than Hannah's. And while Hannah's ears had never been pierced, Simone had tiny holes in hers. Other than that, the two girls really did look identical.

"Try this," said Simone. She ran her fingers through her hair, swept it up off her face, and drew it back into a ponytail. Hannah did the same. The girls had exactly the same hairline, but Simone had a slightly more prominent vein in her left temple, and Hannah's eyebrows were just a little more rounded.

They continued to study each other in silence. On closer inspection, Hannah thought she looked a little healthier than Simone. Her own face was fresh and glowing, but Simone had dark rings beneath tired eyes. And although both girls were thin, at certain angles Simone's thinness verged on boniness.

"I don't think anyone could tell us apart," said Hannah at last, "unless they'd memorized the differences."

"And unless we were standing side by side."

"So...what's your story?" Hannah began. "Who are your parents?"

Simone shrugged as she looked at their joint reflections in the mirror. "I don't know that much about my biological family," she admitted. "I was adopted."

"Me too."

The two girls slowly turned to face each other. "Well … I don't know about you," Simone continued, "but I was born on—"

"Wait, let me guess," Hannah interrupted. "The fifteenth of June, 1997."

Simone just nodded.

"You were six weeks old," Hannah continued, "and you were living in an orphanage in—"

"Rio de Janeiro, in Brazil," Simone cut in.

Now it was Hannah's turn to nod. "Me too."

"Then we must be …"

"Identical twins," said Hannah slowly. "But … I'm sure my parents would have told me if I'd had a sister …"

"If they knew …"

Hannah twisted a lock of hair around her finger. "I've always wanted a sister, but it never occurred to me that I actually had one."

"Didn't it? Sometimes I wondered … I had a sense that something was missing. But it never occurred to me that I had a twin."

Once again the girls were silent. "Where are you from?" Hannah asked after a while.

"Melbourne," said Simone.

"Of course! Me too. That's why you saw me at the airport yesterday. What part of Melbourne?"

"North Fitzroy," said Simone. "You?"

"Armadale." Hannah's face broke into a grin. "So we live, like, a twenty-minute drive away from each other?"

"It looks like it. Stranger things have happened," said Simone.

"It's like that movie, *The Parent Trap*," Hannah said.

"Except that *their* parents were still alive, and they split the twins up deliberately."

The girls left the bathroom and sat cross-legged, opposite each other, on Simone's bed.

"We could have gone the rest of our lives without even knowing of each other's existence," Hannah said.

Simone shook her head. "No, I don't think we could have. I believe in Fate, don't you?" Without waiting for an answer, she continued. "You know, I really didn't want to come to this summer school, but now I'm so glad I did."

"You didn't want to come?" Hannah was stunned.

"I'm so sick of dancing," said Simone.

"Then why *did* you come?"

Simone sighed. "No choice," she said finally. "I've been coming every summer for the last four years. I can't remember the last time my mum asked me what *I* wanted. She just books me in."

"Have you told her how you feel?"

"I've tried," said Simone. "But she … she's not a great listener, my mum."

"And your dad?"

Simone shook her head. "It's just me and my mum." Her gaze drifted toward the window and for a moment she seemed someplace far away. "Anyway," she said, snapping back to the present, "it's complicated because my biological mother—or should I say *our* biological mother?—was a dancer."

"*Was* she?" Hannah's heart beat a little faster. "How do you know?"

"My mum told me," said Simone. "It's the one thing she does know about my natural mother."

"But *how* does she know? I mean, my family weren't given any information about my biological parents."

"Well, all I can tell you is that they died in a car accident on the way to the hospital. They were almost there when the car crashed, which is how I survived."

"How *we* survived," Hannah corrected.

"My father... *our* father... was driving. He was killed almost instantly, but they managed to get my mother to the hospital, and I was born by C-section just before she—"

"*We* were born by C-section," Hannah interrupted.

"Yeah, I guess... before she died."

"I still don't see how you know all this. The orphanage didn't tell my parents anything. They said it was against the rules..."

"My mum dragged it out of one of the nurses," Simone explained. "That's why I dance. She sent me to ballet lessons as a way of... honoring my mother's memory, I suppose. And once she discovered I was good at it, she decided that I must have inherited my mother's talent."

"Well, she was right about that. Where do you take classes?"

"The VSD," said Simone.

"The VSD?" Hannah almost squealed with excitement. "The school that every dancer wants to go to?"

"Not *every* dancer," said Simone.

"Don't you like it there?"

Simone shook her head. "I did at first. The thing is, I don't really want to dance anymore. Not as a career. I hate performing. I hate the feeling that I'm being judged. And it's just so tiring. Sometimes," she confided, "I cry from exhaustion."

Hannah just stared at her, wondering how Simone could hate the very thing that she herself craved. She would have given anything to be one of the lucky dancers at the VSD. How wonderful to have the chance to train professionally! But how terrible to be pushed into it. She tried to imagine what it must be like, day after day, to be forced to do one strenuous class after another if it wasn't really what you wanted to do.

"That must be awful," she said.

"You have no idea." Simone gave herself a little shake, then glanced at the small alarm clock by the bed. "I've got a jazz class now."

"Already? Has it been an hour?"

"Yeah. Look, I'd better go."

"But...you must be starving," said Hannah. "You haven't had lunch yet, have you?"

"I'll grab an apple from the Caff on my way to class. How about you? Are you hungry?"

"Nope," said Hannah. "I ate on the plane."

Simone gazed at Hannah as though trying to memorize her features. "I still can't believe you're here and you're my roommate. Why don't you unpack while I'm gone?" She paused in the doorway. "I wish I didn't have to leave now, but they do a roll call."

Hannah regarded her twin with sympathy. "You really don't want to go?"

Simone sighed, her face a mixture of exhaustion and sheer lack of enthusiasm. "I really don't," she said.

"Well, you know, I haven't registered yet..." The twinkle in Hannah's eye was unmistakable.

"You mean...?"

"Yeah," said Hannah. "I could go in your place."

"Would you?"

"Why not? I can't wait to start dancing." Hannah had already flung open her suitcase and was tossing her dancewear onto the bed. "Where's the class?"

"The same studio I was in before."

Hannah pulled on jazz shorts and a matching top.

"Wait!" said Simone. "Won't it look strange if I've changed my clothes?"

Hannah shrugged. "Not necessarily. Lots of people change between classical and jazz. They're such different styles."

"I guess..."

Hannah tied the laces on her jazz shoes. "How long is the class?"

"An hour and a half, but—"

"See you in an hour and a half, then." And before Simone could finish the sentence, Hannah had gone.

# seven

After Hannah had left, Simone's mind was in a whirl. Had she really discovered an identical sister? Instinct told her she had, for a jolt of recognition had shot through her when she'd first glimpsed Hannah at the airport, and then again today.

But she had no memory at all of a sister, and a barrage of emotions overwhelmed her. On the one hand, discovering she had a twin was the most wonderful thing that could happen to her. But the reunion with Hannah had been so unexpected, so...surreal, it was hard to believe it had happened at all. And now that Hannah had gone off to class, it seemed like she might have been a kind of mirage—a trick of the mind.

Simone undressed and stood under the shower, silently rejoicing in the fact that she'd finished her classes for the rest of the day. How lucky that Hannah had offered to go in her place. Simone would never have had the temerity to suggest it herself, even if she'd thought of the idea. It took someone courageous to break the rules.

Maybe some of Hannah's courage would rub off on her

if they spent enough time together … which made Simone wonder, why hadn't they? Why had she and Hannah been separated?

Could Harriet have known that Simone had a twin? Simone doubted it. Harriet had her faults, but she wasn't devious or secretive. Still, might she know more than she'd ever let on?

As she toweled herself dry, Simone realized she wouldn't get the rest she craved. Her head was too full of questions. With the towel wrapped firmly around her, she padded barefoot into the room where Hannah's open suitcase revealed a jumble of clothes.

Simone reached for her handbag, which lay at the back of the wardrobe, and rummaged about for her mobile phone. She was about to key in her mother's number when she changed her mind.

Harriet would want to know *why* Simone was asking— why now, after all these years?—and Simone didn't want to tell her. The discovery that she had an identical twin was still so new that she wanted to keep it to herself for a little while longer. She needed time to digest the relationship, and although—or perhaps because—they'd only just met, she felt possessive of Hannah and didn't want to share her. Oh, she'd tell her mother eventually—but not just yet.

She replaced the phone, then put on a pair of shorts and a T-shirt and went outside, reveling in the unfamiliar feeling of independence and anonymity. And as she strolled along the tree-lined streets, all she could think of was Hannah.

———

Hannah sprinted across the lawn, and by the time she slipped into the studio, she was a little breathless. Most of Simone's class was already there, sitting on the floor in groups of two or three or lounging at the barre.

"Hey, Simone." A tall girl with dark hair and a friendly smile was approaching her. She had smooth skin the color of honey and the kind of natural poise that Hannah envied. "Where were you?" she asked. "I was hoping we could have lunch together, but you disappeared."

"Oh, I'm...uh..." *Not Simone*, she'd been about to say, before remembering to keep that information to herself. "I'm sorry," she said instead. "I had to call my mum. She kept me on the phone forever."

Just then an older woman—mid-thirties, perhaps— entered the room. "Hello. I'm Stacy Greene, and I'll be your jazz teacher."

The clusters of dancers dispersed as each student found a place in the center of the studio.

Stacy Greene held a folder and a pen. "I'll just tick off your names before we begin. It won't take long."

The teacher clearly knew some of the dancers from previous years, for instead of pronouncing their names as an inquiry, she murmured things like, "Ah, there you are, Liam," or "Sam, great to see you again." Now she gave Hannah a warm smile of recognition. "Ah, the lovely Simone."

Hannah took a deep breath and smiled back.

———

Thanks to her training at Armadale Dance and her natural talent, Hannah held her own in class. She'd been learning jazz since she was eight years old, and it was a style that came easily to her. It didn't require the restraint or strict discipline of classical ballet, and Hannah threw herself into it, confident that in this one style, at least, she was every bit as advanced as the others.

After the warm-up exercises, performed to an old Michael Jackson number, the dancers learned the steps that would form part of the routine for the Candance concert. Hannah picked up the choreography quickly and easily.

As she was leaving the studio, still buzzing from the fast routines, a boy with dark hair and an impish smile bumped into her. "Ah, the lovely Simone."

Hannah laughed at his impersonation of the teacher. "And you are?"

"Tom. Two roll calls and you still don't know my name? I'm gutted."

"He really is," said the boy behind him. "You're all he's talked about the entire day."

"Thanks, Liam," said Tom, elbowing the taller boy in the ribs. "So," he said, turning to Hannah, "where are you from?"

# eight

Simone returned to the dorm room happier and more relaxed. Hannah, now showered and dressed in a tank top and shorts, was pulling a wide-toothed comb through her long wet hair.

Simone flashed her a complicit smile. "I still can't believe you're really here. After you left for class, I kept thinking that maybe I'd imagined you. But then I'd see your suitcase, and your clothes, and—"

"Imagine how *I* felt," Hannah said. "I mean, this morning I didn't even know you existed, and by this afternoon I was pretending to *be* you. And everyone just assumed I was you. It was really weird."

"So, no one suspected?"

Hannah shook her head as she slipped her feet into a pair of thongs.

Simone perched on the end of her bed. "Were you tempted to tell?"

"Kind of, but unless you'd been standing right beside me, I'm not sure anyone would have believed it. Speaking of which, did you call home while I was gone? Did you tell your mum?"

Simone shook her head. "I was going to, but at the last minute I changed my mind. I guess I wanted to ... keep it to myself for a while."

Hannah grinned. "I know. Me too." She flopped onto the bed beside Simone. "But there's a part of me that wants to tell everyone."

"It's just so ... *huge*," said Simone. "This sudden discovery that I've got a sister. And I've got this silly, superstitious sort of feeling that if I tell anyone, it will turn out not to be real, and you'll suddenly vanish ... "

Hannah laughed. "Don't worry. I'm not going anywhere."

Simone smiled. "So how was the class?"

"Fabulous. By the way, there's this guy who likes you."

"Who?"

"Dark-haired guy. Kind of cute. His name is Tom. Hey, you're blushing."

"He caught me staring at him," said Simone.

"Do you like him, then?"

Simone gave a noncommittal shrug. "Do you?"

"Not my type," said Hannah. "But go for it. Apparently he's had his eye on you all day ... I bet he'll talk to you tomorrow."

"God, don't mention tomorrow," said Simone, her shoulders slumping. "It was so great not having to go to class this afternoon. I felt like I was really on holiday."

A look—part sympathy, part confusion—crossed Hannah's

face. "You make it sound like such drudgery. Is that really how you think of dancing?"

"I wish I didn't, but..." Simone trailed off. "Maybe it will be different with you here," she continued. "Maybe I'll forget how tired I am of dancing. I wonder how everyone will react when they see us together," she added, brightening.

"Oh, but I won't be in your class. I'm pretty sure I've been placed in the level below."

"Well, that sucks."

"Yeah, I know." Hannah sat up and crossed her legs, her chin cupped in the palm of her hand. "Listen," she said, her voice taking on a conspiratorial tone. "Why don't I just email the office and say I've broken my leg and can't make it to summer school after all? Then I can go to all your classes, and you can have the rest you wanted."

"You think we could get away with it for three whole weeks?" Simone asked, frowning.

"Oh, wouldn't it be great if we could!" Hannah jumped up and spun around the room, but her face fell as she came to a wobbly stop at the foot of the bed. "No, I guess you're right. It was one thing getting away with it in your jazz class—I've always been pretty good at jazz—but ballet? I'd give myself away within the first thirty seconds. I'm not nearly as well trained as you."

"How long have you been learning?" asked Simone.

"Since I was five. And I'm probably the best dancer at my school. But the best dancer at Armadale Dance isn't as good as the worst dancer at the VSD."

"How do you know?" said Simone.

"Everyone knows how hard it is to get into the VSD. And remember, I saw you in class before. Your *fouettés* were perfect. Mine are hopeless."

"Show me," said Simone.

Hannah jettisoned the thongs, then, barefoot, took a preparation in fourth position and began the turn. Unable to sustain it, she kept collapsing and starting again. "See? Hopeless!"

"You need a stronger center," said Simone. "Just think *center* all the time. Focus on the rise, not the *plié*, so that instead of thinking *down*, and *down*, and *down*, you think *up*, and *up*, and *up* . . . that's it. Much better. Now, try it on pointe."

"That'll be harder," said Hannah.

"Nope. Easier, actually." Simone smiled as Hannah ransacked her suitcase.

By the time Hannah found her scuffed and somewhat tatty pointe shoes, the floor was virtually hidden beneath a mess of clothes. "I should probably get new ones," she said, winding the ribbon around one slender ankle, "but I thought these would do." As she tied the ribbon on the other foot, it snapped off the shoe. "Rats! Have you got a needle and thread?"

Simone shook her head. "No, but you can try my shoes." A moment later she was handing Hannah the pink satin shoes she'd been wearing earlier. They looked much newer than Hannah's.

Hannah slipped her bare feet into Simone's pointe shoes. They were a perfect fit.

"Keep them," said Simone.

"But they're in such good condition. They'll be completely worn out by the end of summer."

"They'd be just as worn out if I used them myself."

"I guess..." Hannah tied the ribbons firmly and carefully. "Awesome," she said. "Maybe while I'm wearing them, some of your skill will rub off on me."

Simone smiled. "You've got enough of your own. Come on, show me some *fouettés* on pointe."

Hannah started to limber up, pointing and flexing one foot at a time. Then she stood up and started the difficult turn.

"Great," said Simone. "You're wrong if you think you don't have skill. Look how quickly you've improved."

"Still, I'm nowhere near as good as you."

"Maybe not," said Simone, "but you're better than some of the girls who've been placed in my class."

"Really?"

"Uh-huh. Admin never gets all the placements exactly right. They place you according to what you tell them when you fill in the form."

"Still," said Hannah, "if I go into class pretending to be you, won't your teacher expect me to be as good as you?"

Simone shrugged. "It's not like she knows me that well. She's new this year. She only met me this morning. And dancers are never that consistent. They have good days and bad days."

Hannah spun into a series of *chaînés*, and Simone watched, impressed. "You're better than you think," she said. "You *should* be in the highest level."

As if to prove her wrong, Hannah came crashing into Simone, and together they fell onto Simone's bed, laughing. "The highest level, huh?" said Hannah. "You really think so?"

# nine

It took Hannah less than two minutes to set up a new hot-mail account in her mother's name. As she sat at the desk, typing on her laptop, Simone pulled up the other chair and sat beside her.

Hannah began:

*To: j.jones@candance.com.au*
*From: vanessasegal@hotmail.com*

*Dear Ms. Jones,*

*Unfortunately, my daughter Hannah has broken her leg and will be unable to attend the Candance summer school after all.*

"Now what?" asked Hannah.

"I apologize for any inconvenience this may cause," Simone dictated.

"Oh, that's good," said Hannah.

" … and hope she will be able to join you next year."

Hannah typed as Simone dictated, then added another sentence of her own.

*The fees have already been paid in full, but it would be great if you could refund at least some of the money …*

"Hmm! Try: I will understand if you are unable to provide any refunds at this late stage," Simone suggested.

"Right," said Hannah. She deleted the last line and began again.

*The fees have already been paid in full, but I will understand if you are unable to provide any refunds at this late stage.*

"However," Simone continued, "if you were able to return at least some of the money, I would be extremely grateful."

"Okay, but remember we have to get the money put into my account, not sent as a check to my home address."

"Right," said Simone. "How about, 'If it is possible to provide a partial refund, the best way to do so would be via direct deposit'?"

"That's perfect."

Hannah typed in the sentence, then added:

*My account details are as follows:*

"Wait, I'll have to check." She stood up, unearthed her purse from beneath a pile of clothes, and brought it over to the desk.

*Bank: Westpac*
*BSB: 033 059*
*Account number: 647280*
*Account name: Segal*

"Just Segal?" said Simone. "No first name? Won't that look suspicious?"

"Maybe, but there's no way I can tell her the account is in my name. That *would* look suspicious." Hannah paused. "Sincerely, Best Wishes, or Kind Regards?"

"Kind regards," said Simone. "But you forgot the part about not phoning."

"Oh, right."

*The best way to contact me is through this email address, as my phone is currently out of order.*

"Anything else?" asked Hannah.

"Thank you for your understanding," said Simone.

*Thank you for your understanding.*
*Kind regards,*
*Vanessa Segal*

Hannah stopped typing and looked at Simone. "Are you absolutely sure you want to do this?"

Simone nodded. "Absolutely."

Hannah pressed *send*, then turned to her newfound sister and grinned. "You do realize, don't you, that if we get busted, we're done for?"

Simone turned pale.

"Don't worry, Simone. We'll just have to make sure that doesn't happen."

———————

"We must be insane," said Simone as she watched Hannah pick up a bundle of clothes and shove them haphazardly into the wardrobe.

"It'll be fine," said Hannah, "as long as no one realizes." She tipped the remaining contents of her suitcase onto her bed.

"So we can't tell *anyone*," said Simone. "Agreed?"

"Agreed," said Hannah. She gave the suitcase a final shake and a bottle of shampoo rolled onto the floor.

"Simone?" called a voice from outside the room. A loud knocking followed. "Simone, are you there?"

"It's Sam," Simone mouthed to Hannah.

"Let her in," whispered Hannah. "I'll wait in the bathroom." Hannah withdrew into the steamy bathroom and Simone went to open the door.

Sam entered, still dressed in her jazz shorts, long hair piled carelessly on top of her head. "Who were you talking to?" she asked.

"Uh … no one."

"Oh, I thought I heard voices." She stepped around the open suitcase and flung herself down on Hannah's bed. "God, it's a mess in here. How come you haven't finished unpacking? I thought you were a stickler for neatness."

"I was," said Simone. "I mean, I used to be," she added

quickly, trying not to let her gaze slide toward the bathroom door. Where would Hannah hide, she wondered, if Sam wanted to use the—

"So I'll save you a spot in the dining room," Sam was saying.

"Sorry, what?" Simone realized she hadn't been listening.

"I said I'll save you a spot for dinner."

"Uh, I…" Dinner with Sam was out of the question— Simone had been counting on spending the evening with Hannah. "Sorry, but I seem to have developed this hideous stomach bug. I really don't think I'll be able to eat."

Sam tried to mask her disappointment. "Lunch tomorrow?"

"Ah, sure…lunch tomorrow. I'll see you in class in the morning."

"Okay, then." Sam gave Simone a little wave goodbye. "Feel better," she added, shooting Simone a look of sympathy as she shut the door.

"Phew!" said Hannah, emerging from the bathroom. "It's like a sauna in there."

———

After Sam left, the girls drew up a list of rules:

- Wait until the other dancers have gone to dinner before leaving the room.

- Never leave the room together. Always leave a minimum ten-minute interval.

- Try to look as unalike as possible.

- Never be seen on campus together.

- Never be seen within a two-kilometer radius of Candance together.

- Arrive at restaurants separately.

- Take the table furthest from the window.

- Take the table in the darkest corner.

- Tell no one. Tell no one. TELL NO ONE.

---

Hannah gave Simone a quick hug and left the room. Simone watched her go, thinking how good she looked in her denim shorts and sleeveless top, long hair bouncing around her shoulders. Then she changed into a knee-length dress, tied her hair in a ponytail, put on a pair of large, dark sunglasses, and completed the transformation with a floppy sunhat. Checking that a full ten minutes had passed since Hannah left, Simone stepped out into the corridor and shut the door.

Outside the dorm, the sun was just beginning to set. Simone picked up her pace, eager to reach the restaurant quickly. For one thing, she'd eaten so little all day that her stomach was rumbling. For another, she was missing Hannah already. It was hard to believe she could miss someone she'd only met that day, but maybe that's the way it was with twins. There was a special bond...

With Simone's instructions to guide her, Hannah had no trouble finding the Italian bistro. Romeo's was about a hundred meters from the main road and suitably inconspicuous, tucked away behind a tall hedge of native pines.

Sitting alone, at one of the small tables that was covered in a red-and-white checked cloth, Hannah thought about all that had happened in the last twenty-four hours. This time yesterday she was still in Melbourne, distraught at having had her flight to Canberra cancelled, and today she was waiting for a sister she'd never even known she had. The last few hours had gone by so quickly that she'd barely had a chance to take it all in.

A middle-aged waiter brought her a glass of water and placed it on the table with a flourish. Hannah smiled and thanked him, then pulled out her phone and checked the new account she'd just set up in Vanessa's name. Sure enough, there was a new message in the inbox.

*To: vanessasegal@hotmail.com*
*From: j.jones@candance.com.au*

*Dear Ms. Segal,*

*I'm so sorry that Hannah can't join us this summer at Candance, and I wish her a speedy recovery.*
*Unfortunately, we are unable to refund the cost of accommodation, but we will refund the remaining fee for full-board catering.*

*Under the circumstances, we can also provide a full refund for the three weeks of full-time dance tuition, minus the $60 nonrefundable enrollment fee and the initial $100 deposit. Your refund will therefore be $900 for the dance tuition. You will also receive a catering refund of $560, for a total sum of $1,460.*

*Please allow five working days for the funds to be deposited into your chosen account.*

*Best Wishes,*
*Jocelyn Jones*

# ten

"*One thousand, four hundred and sixty dollars?*" Simone let out a little shriek. "You've got to be kidding me."

"Nope, see for yourself."

Simone whipped off her hat and sunglasses and shoved them into her enormous tote bag, then took the iPhone from Hannah and read the email. "It's a fortune," she said. "We can't possibly keep it. It's your parents' money. And you've got no idea how hard my mum works to pay for—"

"For what? A course you didn't want to do in the first place?"

Simone shook her head. "Don't you get it? I feel like a thief."

"Well, you shouldn't feel that way. It's right that the program refund the money if only one of us is doing the course. And you're not stealing anything by living in the dorm because that part's fully paid and non-refundable. You'll need at least some of this money to pay for all the meals you won't be having on campus. Like this one," she added. "Besides, you can always pay your mother back. And my parents are still getting their money's worth!" She stopped talking as the pot-bellied waiter approached their table with a basket of sliced Italian bread.

"Ah, I see your friend has arrived," he said to Hannah. He glanced at Simone, then did a double-take. His head swiveled from one to the other and back again. "Identical twins," he declared, his eyes growing wider.

"Shhhh," said Hannah in a stage whisper. "We're trying to be incognito."

The waiter laughed. "What can I get you?"

"I'll have the spaghetti marinara, please," said Simone.

"And I'll have the vegetarian penne." Hannah waited till he was out of earshot, then leaned closer to Simone. "Are you sure you won't be missed in the communal dining room?"

Simone shook her head. "I told you, it's cafeteria style. No one ever bothers checking who's there and who's not."

A drinks waiter arrived with two glasses of something cold and pale yellow.

"Lemon squash. It's on the house."

"Really?"

"*Si*. For some reason, the boss liked the look of you." He paused and turned from one to the other, then grinned in delight.

The girls burst out laughing when he left.

"Here's to three weeks of swapping identities," Hannah said.

"And getting to know each other," said Simone.

They clinked glasses, and drank.

The twins talked nonstop all through dinner. It didn't take them long to find out that although they'd both been raised in Melbourne, their lives were completely different. Simone had been raised a Catholic. Hannah had been raised a Jew. Simone had always gone to public schools. Hannah attended Carmel College, a private Jewish one. Simone lived in a tiny house. Hannah lived in a fairly large one.

"I can't imagine living with just one other person," Hannah was saying. "It must be quiet at your place."

"It must be noisy at yours."

Back at the dorm, the girls logged onto Facebook and showed each other their photos. Hannah's were a mix of family and friends, while Simone's were mainly of her classmates at the VSD. The conversation continued long after they had gone to bed; Simone lay on her left side, facing Hannah in across the room, and Hannah lay on her right side, facing Simone.

"So you *never* had a dad?" Hannah was saying.

"Never," said Simone.

"That's sad."

"Is it? I'm not sure if you can miss what you never had … and there's something romantic about being so in love … "

"But it must have been awful for your mum when her fiancé died."

"Yeah … I guess that's why she adopted me. To fill the gap."

"But that was over fifteen and a half years ago. And she's been single all that time?"

"At least she's got me."

"What does she do?" asked Hannah.

"She works for an insurance company. What about your parents?"

"My mum's a doctor and my dad's a publisher. Ever heard of Seagull Press?"

"Of course."

"Well, that's us. Segal—Seagull."

"Oh, that is *so* cool … "

"My dad's always trying to get me to read. Every time he publishes a new book, he brings me a copy. I've got this huge pile of unread novels in my room."

"Oh, lucky lucky you. I wish someone brought *me* books. I mean, not that I'd have time to read them, but I wish I did. I love reading."

"Do you? Ha! My dad would love you." Hannah was quiet for a moment. "Maybe he got the wrong twin." She said it lightly, but suddenly it seemed like a real possibility. "I must be a disappointment to him," she added softly.

"You couldn't be," Simone assured her. "If anyone's a disappointment, it's me."

"You? Why you?"

"The only thing my mum wants is for me to be a dancer. Imagine how disappointed she'll be when she finds out I won't be."

"Hmm … my parents see dance as just a hobby." Hannah yawned and closed her eyes.

"It's weird," said Simone. "I got the mother who wants me to dance. You got the father who wants you to read."

Hannah said nothing. She had slipped into sleep.

––––––––––

Hannah lay in a fetal position, her right hand making a loose fist as if she'd been grasping something and had lost her grip. Lying with her left hand curled up by her face, Simone was the mirror image of her sister.

But while Hannah slept on undisturbed, Simone began to toss and turn in the midst of an unpleasant dream.

*"Mum, I told you. She's my sister. We're identical twins."*

*"Oh, Simone! What next?"*

*"But can't you see the resemblance? LOOK at her."* *Simone's voice was becoming desperate.*

*"Look at who, Simone?"*

*"At Hannah."* *By now Simone was close to tears.* *"Please, Mum. She's standing right…"* *But when Simone turned to the spot where Hannah had stood just a moment before, there was no one there.*

Simone stirred restlessly. "She *was* there," she muttered out loud. Woken by the sound of her own voice, Simone sighed and opened her eyes.

Silvery moonlight seeped through the skimpy curtains and the looming shadows became more distinct as Simone's night vision slowly returned. What had she been dreaming? For a second, she couldn't remember. Then she glanced over at Hannah and it all came back—it was a variation of a dream she'd already had three times that night, and each time she'd woken up deeply disturbed.

Once again she glanced at Hannah, who was fast asleep and breathing deeply. Simone wondered if she too was having bad dreams, but Hannah looked peaceful.

Simone closed her eyes. Despite the unsettling thoughts in her mind, tiredness overwhelmed her, and at last she slept.

# eleven

Hannah looked around the busy Caff. Some of the dancers were sitting at tables, taking their time over breakfast. Others grabbed a piece of toast or fruit and ate on the run, while there were those who downed a glass of juice and left carrying a container of yogurt or a hardboiled egg still in its shell.

What would Simone like for breakfast? Hannah had left her fast asleep, even though she was dying to wake her. It had been so amazing waking up in the same room as her very own sister.

Simone had said that breakfast at Candance was the best meal of the day, and judging by the generous buffet, Hannah guessed that must be true. There were different kinds of cereal, bowls of fruit, two sorts of toast, hard- or soft-boiled eggs, hot porridge, baked beans, containers of flavored yogurt, and miniature packets of butter, Vegemite, and assorted jam.

Hannah wrapped two slices of toast in a napkin and popped some butter and Vegemite into her bag, along with two hard-boiled eggs, an apple, a pear, and a container of yogurt. She picked up two teaspoons and two knives, glanced quickly around to make sure no one was watching, and then slid them into the bag as well. It was probably against the rules, but she had every intention of returning them when Candance ended.

Sam and Liam were sitting at a table by the window, engrossed in conversation. Luckily they hadn't seen her yet, and she was careful not to catch their eye as she slipped outside.

Simone was still asleep when Hannah returned, and Hannah tiptoed quietly across the room. As she silently unpacked their breakfast onto the desk, a knife fell clattering onto the floor. Simone woke with a start.

"Shhh … sorry. Go back to sleep."

Simone sat up, rubbing her eyes. "It's okay. I'm awake." She looked a little disoriented and her voice was croaky as she said, "What's that?"

"I brought us some breakfast."

"I don't think I'm entitled to any, and *you're* supposed to eat in the Caff."

"Hang on a minute," said Hannah. "Why aren't you entitled to any?"

"We're getting a refund, remember?" said Simone. "The cost of full-board catering is being returned. So if I eat here, I'm stealing from Candance."

"Wrong," said Hannah. "Full board means three meals a day, remember? And since I'll be eating dinner out, with you … two breakfasts plus one lunch equals three meals total, right?"

"Right," said Simone.

"Well, there you go."

Simone got up, brushed her teeth, and slowly buttered a piece of toast. "Actually, it's probably a good thing you brought me food, because my mum didn't give me much spending money."

"Why not?"

"She paid for full board, remember? So why would I need it?"

"Well, take my bankcard," said Hannah. "Here's my PIN." She scribbled a four-digit number on a scrap of paper and handed the card and the number to Simone. "There's enough in there for food even before the refund gets deposited."

"I can't take your money," said Simone.

"Yes you can," Hannah said, through a mouthful of egg on toast. "And it's not really *my* money, is it? If it were you my parents had adopted, it could just as easily be yours."

Simone looked uncomfortable but took the card. "Thanks," she said. "How come you've got your own bank account, anyway?"

Hannah shrugged. "Pocket money, birthday money, Hanukkah money…" She glanced at the clock. "Anyway, gotta go, or I'll be late for warm-up!"

———

Miss Roth's voice rose and fell in a steady rhythm as she marked out the exercise. "*Demi plié* and stretch, *demi plié* and stretch, *grand plié* and stretch, and rise and turn." Hannah stood at the barre watching, her hands sketching the prescribed movements of the legs and feet. She was nervous, but in a good way. This was her first ballet lesson at Candance, and it was what she'd been waiting for. It was why she'd spent months trying to convince her parents to let her enroll. It was her best chance to improve as a dancer, because training in classical ballet with the top teachers in the country was the most wonderful training a dancer could get.

Hannah had been learning ballet for nearly ten years. She was good, but coming from Armadale Dance, she just wasn't sure she was good enough. Could she really fool Miss Roth into thinking she was Simone, who'd trained at the prestigious, entry-by-audition-only VSD?

She placed one hand lightly on the barre, the music began, and Miss Roth strode up and down the length of the studio, watching the dancers. "Don't race the music. Fill it. Stretch the movement. That's it. Lovely."

The class moved on to another exercise, and another. "Peel the foot off the floor and into *retiré*," Miss Roth was saying. "Bring the leg into an *attitude derrière*, stretch it out into an *arabesque* and carry it to the side... Don't drop the knee." She passed from one end of the barre to the other, making minor adjustments to the dancers' positions. She stopped beside Hannah, looked her up and down, and moved on to the girl in front.

*I've done it,* thought Hannah. *She hasn't noticed a thing.*

Just then Miss Roth turned back and caught Hannah's eye. "Square hips, please, Simone. And pull in that rib cage.

# twelve

Bag slung over her shoulder, sunhat and dark glasses on her head, Simone trotted along the footpath. She was planning to spend the day at the local pool and was on her way to the bus stop, but swimming was the last thing on her mind. Instead, she was thinking about Hannah's dad and the fascinating fact that he was a publisher. She imagined meeting him. They'd talk about books and writing, and he'd tell her all about publishing and the famous authors he'd met and worked with. Maybe she'd have a chance to meet them too ...

In the photos Hannah had shown her the night before, the whole Segal family looked warm and good-humored. Brown-skinned Adam seemed cheeky and funny and had a wiry, athletic build. Hannah's mom Vanessa was small and neat, and often had a kind of half-smile on her face. And Manfred ... Manfred looked like the kind of dad you'd want to have. He was a large man, his smile open and friendly, and he appeared to have an insatiable appetite not only for food but for life.

What would her life have been like if she'd had Manfred for a dad? Or if she'd even *had* a dad? It wasn't something Simone had ever really thought about, but since meeting Hannah her mind was all over the place, filled with questions she couldn't even begin to answer.

She tried to imagine herself and Hannah as tiny infants—two identical baby girls in a Brazilian orphanage.

Was there even any proof that she and Hannah were identical twins? Or was it possible that their history and identical looks were just coincidence?

It would be so much easier to tell their parents, when the time came, if they could prove it was true. Well, perhaps they could...

She'd once seen a program on TV about DNA testing. It was mostly used to resolve paternity issues, or to determine whether a certain person had committed a crime. And it could identify people who'd died over a hundred years ago. Maybe it could also confirm whether she and Hannah were identical twins.

The bus stop was still a little farther down the street, but Simone retraced her steps and headed to the public library instead.

Once inside, she looked around. A sign on the information desk said *Wi-Fi Internet Available*. Soon, sitting at a designated computer, she opened a search engine and entered the words *DNA Testing Identical Twins*.

Within fifteen minutes, Simone knew the following facts:

- Identical twins have identical DNA.

- Identical twins, formed when a fertilized egg splits, are the *only* people in the world with identical DNA.

- Although identical twins have the same genotype (DNA), they have different phenotypes.

- Phenotype determines traits such as fingerprints and certain aspects of physical appearance, and are a product of the way the individual's genes interact with the environment both within the uterus and throughout the individual's life.

- Dogs can't distinguish between identical twins.

- DNA testing cannot distinguish between identical twins, but a simple fingerprint can.

Simone returned to the search engine and typed in the words *DNA Testing Canberra Australia.*

This time a list of businesses appeared and Simone clicked on the first link: *fastcheckDNA.com.au.* In large print at the top of the site were the words *DNA Testing Australia Wide,* and in a smaller font below, the heading *Paternity Testing: For peace of mind, be sure who is the father of your child.*

Checking some other links, Simone found websites for DNA Australia, Gene Track, and DNA Identity. All seemed to offer similar services at comparable prices. All advertised paternity testing and none mentioned testing for identical twins.

She returned to the Fast Check website and sent an email to the contact address:

*To Whom It May Concern,*

*Could you tell me whether you test for identical twins?*

*Thanks,*
*Simone*

The reply from Fast Check was almost immediate:

*Hello Simone,*

*Yes, we can do testing that will determine if you are identical twins. The cost is $360 and the DNA is collected from a mouth swab. I have attached the application form and as soon as you have returned it to us, we will send you a mouth swab collection kit. Alternatively, you can phone the office and we will take your application over the phone.*

*Payment is due with the return of the collection kit.*

*Yours sincerely,*
*Julianne Barnes MSC (Hons)*
*Director Fast Check DNA*

With a surge of excitement, Simone rang the number provided at the bottom of the email and gave the office her name, birth date, and Candance address. Then she switched off the computer, left the library, and wandered down the street to a nearby café.

As she sipped hot chocolate with a dash of cream—a treat her mother would never approve of—Simone remembered the disturbing dreams she'd had the night before.

*If I have proof that we're identical twins*, she thought, *no one will ever be able to tell me that Hannah's not real.*

---

"Why waste money on a DNA test?" Hannah asked, when Simone suggested using Hannah's credit card to make the payment. "I mean, isn't it obvious we're identical twins?" She watched as Simone slid easily into the splits, her hips square, her posture perfect.

"To us," said Simone, raising one arm and bending over her outstretched leg with enviable elegance. "It's obvious to us. But don't you think it will be easier to tell our parents if we've got the proof?"

"I guess," said Hannah. "Yeah, okay."

Simone's torso swept the floor as she changed direction, reminding Hannah of what had inspired her to dance in the first place. Simone really did move beautifully. Even a simple thing, like lifting an arm into fifth position, was transformed into an act of grace when Simone did it. *She doesn't know,* thought Hannah. *She doesn't how amazing she looks, what a gift she has.*

Simone flipped onto her stomach and pulled one foot up over her head, her back strong and superbly arched.

"You won't really give up dancing, will you?" Hannah asked. "I mean, look at you."

"This isn't dancing, it's stretching," said Simone. "To me, stretching's like breathing."

"Isn't dancing like breathing?" Hannah asked.

"Not anymore." Simone stood up and came to sit beside Hannah on her bed.

Hannah couldn't let it go. "I get that dancing's tiring. I get that you really need a break. And it's your right not to dance, and I fully respect that … but Sim, if I could dance as well as you, I'd want to show the world … "

"I used to feel like that," Simone agreed. "It's not that I don't like dancing. If I could do it just for myself … if I could dance alone in a studio, that might be different. I'd be dancing for me. When you're on your own, there's a purity about dance. It becomes a kind of … meditation. But as soon as someone else is watching, there's this weight of expectation. It ruins everything."

The girls were quiet for a while, each wrapped up in private thoughts.

"You didn't tell me what else you did today," said Hannah at last, "besides finding out about DNA. You weren't bored, were you?"

"Bored?" Simone almost laughed at the question. "I felt free. For the first time in years."

# thirteen

"You don't remember him, do you?" Sam said to Hannah while they were eating lunch on the lawn the following day.

Hannah frowned and shook her head. Though Sam was interesting and friendly and great company, she had an annoying habit of referring to events that Hannah knew nothing about. Now, for instance, she was talking about some guy who'd been at Candance the year before. Hannah thought it best to simply admit she didn't remember. "What did you say he looked like again?"

"Tall, curly hair … you said he was cute."

"Did I? Well, don't forget it's been a year."

"Still …" said Sam, her tone accusing, "I'd never forget a guy who liked me. I mean, not that many of them do," she added, blushing.

"I'm sure loads of them do," Hannah jumped in, grateful for the chance to steer the conversation away from herself. "You're smart and gorgeous, and tall …"

"Too tall," said Sam.

"And a wonderful dancer ..."

"Too tall for a partner ..."

"In a traditional ballet company, maybe. Still, don't you want to do more experimental stuff?"

"Yeah, but it'd be nice to think I had a choice. What kind of dancing do you want to do?"

"Everything," said Hannah. "I think I'd get bored with just one style. I want to audition for *So You Think You Can Dance* when I finish school.

"If it's still on," said Sam. "I'm so over that show." She unwrapped her sandwich and regarded it with a distinct lack of enthusiasm. "You'd think they'd have the imagination to change the menu from time to time. It's been the same for years."

Hannah was already chomping. "Mine's pretty good," she said through a mouthful of sandwich.

"Messy, though," said Sam. "You've got beetroot dribbling down your chin."

"Have I?" Hannah laughed, then noticed Tom and Liam strolling toward them.

"Mind if we join you?" Liam plunked himself down on the grass, and Tom grinned at Hannah.

"Sam's right," said Tom. "You do have beetroot on your chin." He squatted beside her. "If you like, I could wipe it off."

"No way." Hannah punched him lightly on the shoulder.

"Here." Tom handed her the napkin from his own sandwich. "Feeling better?" he asked.

Hannah dabbed at her chin. "Better than what?"

"Sam said you weren't feeling well the last couple of nights; you weren't at the Caff. Eat with us tonight?"

"Can't," said Hannah. "I'm on half-board this year. I have to eat out."

---

Trusty sunhat and large glasses hiding most of her face, baggy pants and an oversized T-shirt concealing her body shape, Simone sat under a large maple, watching as dancers left the School of Dance and headed over to the Caff, soon to emerge again carrying sandwiches in paper bags.

Simone's tummy gave a little rumble. Right now, though, she didn't have time to eat—she had something more important on her mind. A note slipped under her door had informed her that a parcel was waiting for her in the office. Though she'd seen the note at ten in the morning, she couldn't show up at the office when class was in session; she'd had to wait until lunchtime.

In the distance, she could see Hannah and Sam sitting on the grass in the shade of an elm tree, with Tom and Liam strolling over to join them. A moment later, Tom was crouching next to Hannah, and then Hannah was punching him and they were both laughing. She couldn't help feeling a twinge of envy…

It was weird to think she was watching "herself," watching the person the rest of the class was calling "Simone." Weirder still to think the entire class believed that Hannah was her. Didn't they think it strange that a girl who was normally shy and reserved had suddenly become outgoing and gregarious?

Then again, she'd only spent one morning with the other dancers, and even those who remembered her from last year probably wouldn't have thought too much about it. After all, a person could change a lot in a year…

Simone was too far away to hear what they were saying, but the sound of their laughter carried. She was suddenly aware of the contrast between the sense of togetherness the dancers radiated and her own aloneness.

Having been raised an only child, she was used to long stretches of time spent by herself, and generally enjoyed her own company. Now, though, an unexpected pang of loneliness overwhelmed her. Not for the first time, she wondered what it would have been like to have a sister. To have Hannah for company all the time.

She took one last, lingering look at the little group, then reminded herself that right now she was alone by choice, and that sometimes loneliness was the price of freedom. Besides, in just a few hours' time, she'd be with Hannah again…

She resumed her surveillance of the dance building, and when she was sure all the dancers had come out, she stood up and casually strolled across the lawn and up the stairs.

Inside, it was quiet, the studios empty. Simone's footsteps echoed as she walked down the hall to the office. She took off her sunhat and glasses and knocked on the door.

"Come in." Jocelyn Jones looked up and smiled. "Hello, Simone. Did you get my note about your package?"

Simone nodded.

"Your mum must really miss you if she's already sending you goodies from home."

"I guess so," said Simone, thankful that she'd asked for the DNA kit to be sent in an unmarked envelope with no visible return address.

Back in her room, the entire dorm silent and empty, Simone opened the package with trembling fingers. She read the instructions on the enclosed leaflet. Twice through, just to be sure.

The swab was to be taken on an ordinary cotton bud. All she had to do was wipe the tip of the bud against the inside of her cheek, then place it inside a sterile tube. It seemed almost too easy...

––––––––

"Here goes." Simone watched anxiously as Hannah gave the little white stick a final twirl.

"Done," said Hannah. Carefully, she inserted the cotton bud into the clear plastic tube and grinned at her sister. "But I hope it's worth spending three hundred and sixty dollars to find out something we already know."

Simone said nothing, because on some level Hannah was right; they *did* know they were identical twins. They'd conducted their own experiment, consisting primarily of a list of questions to which both had contributed. They'd asked, and answered, separately and in writing so that there could be no cheating, questions like *What is your favorite toothpaste/shampoo/chocolate bar?* (They'd both listed MacLean's, Pantene, and

Coconut Rough.) *What is your lucky number?* (They'd both chosen six.) *Favorite colors?* (Simone had written pink and purple, while Hannah had written purple and pink.)

Yet even though they looked identical and had so much in common, Simone still found it hard to grasp the idea that two genetically identical individuals could be so different.

"If we *are* identical," she said to Hannah, "and our personality differences are caused by our environment, not our genes, then do you think I'd be you if I'd grown up in your family, and you'd be me if you'd grown up in mine?"

Hannah laughed. "I don't think it works that way," she said as she slipped her tube into the padded envelope alongside Simone's. "The changes start within the womb, don't they? Which means by the time we were born, we were already different."

# fourteen

Life at Candance soon slid into an easy routine. Dancing from nine in the morning till four in the afternoon was what Hannah had always longed to do, and she was in her element. If Miss Roth had at first seemed puzzled by the regression in "Simone's" technique, she made up for it by complimenting her on her passion, drive, and artistry. And Hannah was doing just as well in the other classes. Jazz and hip-hop were great fun, classical repertoire was tough but rewarding, and in contemporary dance, she had the chance to create and improvise —something she'd always loved.

Hannah, Sam, Tom, and Liam had become a foursome, and though they took their dancing seriously, they laughed their way through lunchtimes as they listened to anecdotes about each other's lives. Not wanting to contradict anything Simone might have told them, Hannah said nothing about her life back home. But she was so quick to comment on the others' stories, no one seemed to notice that she told none of her own.

The week was drawing to a close. As the four were heading back to class one day, Tom said, "Why don't we ever see you in the evenings, Simone?"

"Yeah," said Sam. "Where do you disappear to?"

"I have a secret life," said Hannah. Sam rolled her eyes and Hannah continued, "It sounds better than saying I promised my mum I'd have early nights."

"You're right, it does," said Liam. "You sad, sad person. That's really lame."

Tom put a hand on Hannah's arm and waited till Sam and Liam had gone on ahead. "You know," he said, leaning toward her, "there's a reason I asked. I'd really like to get to know you."

"You are getting to know me," Hannah said.

Tom shook his head. "Don't think I haven't noticed that you never talk about yourself."

"Maybe I'm not all that interesting," Hannah said.

"No, that's not it." He paused, then added, "Come on, Simone. What are you hiding?"

"Nothing," said Hannah.

"Prove it, then. Let's go out tonight, and you can tell me everything I want to know."

*You've got the wrong sister*, Hannah thought.

But it was the perfect opportunity to set him up with Simone.

———

Engrossed in the story she was reading, Simone hardly noticed the sounds of splashing and laughter. For the first time in her life, she was having the kind of holiday she'd always wanted, spending hours at the local pool, sprawled on a deck chair in the shade of an elm tree with Hannah's Kindle in one hand and a glass of fizzy water in the other. When she wasn't reading, she gazed dreamily over the shining surface of the water or jumped in the pool.

It was wonderful having no Harriet to report to at the end of each day, no one deciding what she ate and watching every mouthful, and, best of all, no one telling her to push her body harder and harder. For the first time in ages, Simone's muscles didn't ache from the minute she got up in the morning till the minute she went to bed at night. Her body felt loose and free.

Finishing the chapter, she set the Kindle aside and re-read the DNA test results that had arrived that morning. She wondered when and how she and Hannah would tell their parents about each other's existence, and imagined a thousand different scenarios. In most of these, the adults were thrilled by the news—after getting over their initial shock.

Still, despite now having proof, Simone couldn't be sure quite how their parents would feel. Would they truly be pleased? Or would they rather not know? When she grew tired of thinking about it, Simone closed her eyes and allowed her mind to wander. It wandered to Tom Delaney and those deep, dark eyes. A tiny half-smile played on her lips as she pictured him. The fact that she didn't know him, and never would, somehow made him more desirable. Thinking about him was definitely preferable to being near him; it was far less threatening—not to mention less embarrassing. And as long as she didn't actually know the guy, nothing could spoil her fantasy of him.

Even so, a part of her wished she could get to know him...

Simone snapped out of her reverie and jumped into the pool. She swam two laps, then climbed out and stood dripping onto the grass, allowing the sun to dry her. It was too hot to stay outside all day, so she headed back to the Candance campus.

Lunchtime was over and the dancers were making their way back to class when Simone arrived. She ducked behind a tree and watched as they entered the building. Among the last to go inside were a couple deep in conversation—Hannah and Tom.

Their heads were close together, as if they'd discovered a world of their own. Once again, Simone felt a stab of envy...

———

Hannah didn't come back to the room for another two hours, leaving Simone free to contemplate what she'd seen. Hannah had said she wasn't interested in Tom, and Simone believed her... but somehow, it hadn't looked that way. So she couldn't help mentioning it the moment Hannah arrived back from class.

"I saw you with Tom. Is something going on between you?"

Hannah swiftly shook her head. "We hang out at lunchtime—Tom and Liam, Sam and I. But I told you before, he's not my type."

"He's mine," said Simone. Her voice was dreamy.

"*Yours*, is he?" Hannah teased.

Simone threw a pillow at her head. "My *type*, you idiot."

"I know that," said Hannah. "That's why I set you up with him. Tonight you're going on a date."

"No way!"

"Yes way. You're meeting him at Koko Black at nine o' clock."

Simone tried to ignore the flutter in her chest. "Don't be stupid! You can't go setting me up on dates."

"Why not?" said Hannah, smiling sweetly. "I'm sure you'd do the same for me."

"What's the point?" said Simone. "I'll never see him again anyway once Candance is over. He probably lives in Queensland or Perth or—"

"Melbourne," said Hannah.

# fifteen

A little after nine that evening, Simone and Tom were sitting at a table for two in Koko Black.

Chin propped in one hand, Tom was looking at Simone as if she were the most fascinating person he'd ever met. He kept up a steady stream of questions and Simone fumbled for intelligent answers under his gaze.

"What do you think of the hip-hop routine?"

A difficult question, considering she'd never seen it. Simone shrugged and didn't answer.

"Do you think the contemporary will come together in time for the concert?"

Once again, she gave a noncommittal shrug. "Maybe," she said, certain he'd think her an idiot incapable of forming a single opinion.

Tom was watching her mouth as she spoke, and her lip trembled. Did she have a chocolate moustache? Simone wiped her lip with the back of her hand.

Tom lifted his cup of Chili Hot Chocolate. "Try this."

Simone took a sip. That way, she could pretend her cheeks were flushed from the chili, not from the way he made her feel. She passed him her own, milder drink. "Here. Try mine."

Tom tasted Simone's Italian Hot Chocolate. "It has no kick."

"It isn't meant to."

Tom began absentmindedly tearing a napkin. "You know," he said, "you're different tonight."

Simone almost choked on the spicy drink. "Different how?" She pushed Tom's cup and saucer toward him.

Tom studied her face and she blushed even harder. "You're kind of... self-conscious. You remind me of the first time I saw you. You were sort of shy that morning. But by the afternoon you were already... I don't know, much more outgoing and confident."

Simone covered her face with her hands and peeped through her fingers. "Do you think we can change the subject now?"

Tom laughed. "Yeah, sorry. So," he said, "how do you like the VSD?"

Simone found herself shrugging yet again. She really didn't want to talk about school.

"It's supposed to be one of the best dance schools in the country," Tom continued. "I guess that means you've got it made."

"Does it?" she asked.

"Well, yeah. I mean, once you've had that sort of training, you'll definitely make it as a dancer."

Simone lifted her own cup and gently blew on the steaming

liquid. "First of all, that isn't true. Dance is an oversupplied industry"—she was quoting Mr. Dixon from school—"and there just aren't that many jobs around. Second of all, I don't actually want to be a professional dancer."

"Seriously? The way you were in jazz today... I've never seen anyone dance with so much passion."

*That was Hannah*, she wanted to say.

"How about you?" she said instead. "Are you planning to be a professional dancer?"

Surprisingly, Tom shook his head. "Dance is what I do for fun. I wouldn't want to see it as something I *had* to do. Actually, Candance is kind of my last fling, dance-wise, I mean. I'll probably give up dancing this fall because I'm starting Year Twelve. Have to really hit the books."

"What do you want to do when you finish school?"

Tom shrugged. "Don't really know. My parents want me to study law. I guess I just want to do well enough to keep my options open. You?"

"Not sure," Simone said. "Maybe work with languages. Or edit books," she added, suddenly thinking of Seagull Press.

"What kind of books? Textbooks, or—"

"Novels," she said without hesitation.

Tom's face lit up. "I like novels too."

Simone gave him a timid smile.

"I like this side of you," he said.

"Which side?" she asked him.

"The shy, serious side. Don't you think it's fascinating how people can be different at different times?"

Simone wiped her mouth carefully on a napkin, avoiding his eyes.

"I'll take these back for a refill," said Tom, reaching for her empty cup. His hand brushed hers and a ping shot through her at the contact.

From the way he was staring at her, she knew that he'd felt it too.

———————

When he came back, they talked about their favorite books. Then somehow his chair had moved closer to hers, and she was too aware of his proximity and the sound of his voice to concentrate on what he was saying.

Later, he reached for her hand as they walked back to the dorm. Unlike the hot, sweaty hands of the boys at school, Tom's hand was warm and dry, and as they strolled down the leafy streets, the air scented with the perfume of jasmine and frangipani, she wished the night would last forever.

Outside the dorm, it was dark and quiet. In the shadow of the darkened building, Tom leaned toward her as if he might kiss her. Time slowed, and for a second she was breathless.

Tom hesitated, brushed the back of his hand across her cheek, and then stepped away. "Good night, Simone. See you tomorrow."

———————

"So," said Hannah. "Are you glad you went?"

"Yes. No. There were moments when we ... but I really don't think I can see him again."

"Why not?" Hannah asked.

It was after midnight and the two girls were lying in their beds, facing each other even though it was too dark to see each other's features.

Simone let out a frustrated sigh. "Because in the end I'd give it away. I mean, how many questions will I have to field before he realizes that I'm not you?"

"What did he ask you?"

"What I thought about the hip-hop dance we did in class and whether I think the contemporary number will come together in time for the concert."

"And what did you say?"

"Not much. God, I felt dumb!"

Hannah chuckled softly. "Don't worry, Sim. That doesn't sound too terrible. And just in case he asks again, the hip-hop dance is wild and the contemporary's a mess." She yawned loudly. "So, did he kiss you?"

"No, he ... I thought he might. But he changed his mind."

Hannah propped herself up on her elbow and tried to see her sister's face. "Did you want him to?" she asked.

Simone turned onto her back and hugged her pillow. "Yes," she whispered.

# sixteen

All through Miss Roth's lesson the following morning, Tom kept throwing Hannah meaningful looks.

Hannah struggled to focus on her dancing. How would she play it, now that she'd supposedly gone out with Tom? She'd only wanted to do something nice for Simone, but perhaps she'd acted too impulsively, arranging the date without thinking things through.

Together with Sam and Liam, she'd always spent most of her day in Tom's company. Now she'd have to find a way to keep her distance from him while still being around him.

What would she do if he tried to kiss her? She'd have to stop him, but what would she say?

When the class was over, Tom came toward her. "I had a really good time last night."

"Yeah, me too."

He put his hands on her shoulders. He was really standing

much too close. Maybe this was how he'd stood with Simone. Hannah squirmed and stepped away.

"I thought..."

"I know. It's just that some things are private," Hannah said quickly, congratulating herself on coming up with the kind of thing Simone might have said. "And I came here to dance."

"That's a weird thing to say, after what you said last night."

"Is it?" said Hannah, wishing she knew what Simone had told him.

Sam and Liam bounded over. "Hi guys," they said.

And Hannah was back to being her bubbly self, laughing and joking while she tried to ignore Tom's bewildered gaze.

At lunchtime, he managed to corner Hannah alone. "So," he said, "tell me the rules."

"I don't want anyone to suspect there's something between us."

"But there *is*, isn't there?"

Hannah sighed. "Maybe, but can we take a rain check?"

"What do you mean?"

"No more dates until we're back in Melbourne? Would that be okay?"

"If that's what you want."

"It is."

"And in the meantime?"

"Let's grab a sandwich and join the others."

---

Hannah threw herself into the hip-hop class in the afternoon and didn't so much as glance at Tom.

"Hey," said Sam after the studio had emptied out, "what's going on with you and Tom?"

"Nothing," said Hannah.

"Really? I heard you two went out last night. But today you were sort of avoiding him."

"No, I wasn't. We hung out at lunchtime. With Liam and you."

"Yeah, he spent the whole time looking miffed and you pretty much ignored him."

The girls took a detour into the changing room to grab their bottles, bags, and towels. "I'm just not ready for a boyfriend," Hannah said. "Maybe it will be different when we're back in Melbourne."

"What if he's given up by then?"

*Good point*, thought Hannah. How would she stall the relationship with Tom while still keeping him interested in Simone?

"Well?" said Sam.

"I guess," said Hannah, exhaling slowly, "that's a chance I'll have to take."

---

Simone had spent most of the morning lying in bed, thinking of Tom. Their date had been fabulous and excruciating in equal measure. If only she had half of Hannah's confidence. If only she hadn't been so awkward and shy.

Replaying the events of the evening before, Simone couldn't help wondering whether it was she or Hannah that Tom really liked. After all, it was Hannah he spent time with every day. Who wouldn't be attracted to Hannah's light-hearted and vivacious nature?

And yet... he hadn't minded when he noticed that Simone seemed different. He'd even said that he liked that about her—the fact that she was shy and serious.

She wondered whether he'd want to date her again. True, she'd given Hannah strict instructions not to accept. Even so, she hoped he'd ask...

At one o'clock, Hannah came back briefly to see Simone before heading off to meet the others in the Caff for lunch.

"How did things go today with Tom?" Simone asked.

"Tricky," said Hannah. "I told him I wanted to put our relationship on hold till we got back to Melbourne, that I came here to dance. He said that was weird, considering what I'd said last night."

"Oh, stupid me," said Simone, emitting a groan.

"Why, what did you tell him?"

"That I didn't want to be a professional dancer."

"Why would you say that," Hannah asked, rolling her

eyes, "when he sees me in the studio every day busting my gut to be the best dancer I can be?"

"I didn't think," said Simone. "I...I wanted him to know the real me."

# seventeen

A few days later, Simone and Hannah were back at Romeo's, the little Italian bistro where they'd first shared a meal. They were digging into a basket of garlic bread while waiting for the large pizza and salad they'd ordered.

"So, we were doing the Dance of the Cygnets," Hannah was saying, "and I went the wrong way. Sam caught it on camera—it was so embarrassing."

Simone laughed as she pictured it. "Yeah, I've done that dance in repertoire. Someone always stuffs up."

"And I really don't see how we're going to nail it with only ten days to go."

"Ten days…" Simone let out a desperate groan. Now that she'd had a taste of freedom, she was dreading the end of summer more than ever, and ten days away seemed far too soon.

"What's wrong, Sim? Hey, don't tell me you're regretting the swap, that you wish you were dancing…"

"God, no," said Simone. "It's not that. This has been

the best holiday ever, and I'm really grateful you're taking my place."

"But?"

"It's such a short-term solution. As soon as summer school's over, it's back to my old life, back to training six days a week at the VSD."

"But why don't you stand up for yourself?" said Hannah, frowning. "Why can't you just tell your mum you won't go back?"

Simone sighed and looked away. "You don't know what it's like to be an only child—especially an only child to a single mother. Your parents have each other, and you, and your younger brother, but my mum—well, she's only got me."

"Then wouldn't she want to know you were happy?"

Simone bit her lip and didn't answer.

The conversation halted momentarily as the waiter delivered their pizza, with its appetizing aroma of garlic and herbs. Hannah slid one slice onto Simone's plate and one onto her own. "Mmm...smells delicious."

Simone said nothing.

"Tell me, Sim," Hannah persisted, "what's the worst that could happen if you told your mum you're sick and tired of the VSD and want to leave?"

Simone imagined her mother's response.

*You only THINK you want to leave.*

*You don't know what you're saying. Dancing's what you always wanted.*

*A million girls would die for a place at the VSD.*

*You don't know how lucky you are.*

*All dancers doubt themselves from time to time. It's just a temporary setback.*

*You must be suffering from PMS. You'll feel differently in a couple of days.*

*You'll always regret it.*

Simone moved the pizza around on her plate. "She'd give me a million reasons why I shouldn't. And she'd be *so* disappointed…"

"But Sim, you have to try."

"I know," said Simone. She dropped her knife and fork on the table and pushed her plate away. "I don't want to go back to the VSD for another day, let alone three more years, but…" She broke off, picked up her glass of water, and sipped. "On the way here, I promised myself that at the end of summer I'd confront my mum, but when I try to see myself actually doing it, I can't. And if I can't do it even in my imagination, what hope have I got of doing it for real? Anyway," she continued, "there's not much point in telling her I want to leave. It's too late to change schools for the coming year. Enrollments closed ages ago."

"You could still *try*," said Hannah.

Tears welled up in Simone's eyes as she faced her sister. "Bottom line, I'm just not brave enough to face my mum."

"You make her sound like some sort of monster."

Simone sighed. "She's not a monster. She's just a woman who's invested her entire life in me."

Hannah took a bite of her pizza and chewed slowly as she studied her sister's gloomy face.

"I'm sorry," said Simone.

"What for?" said Hannah, through a mouthful of food.

"Here I am dragging you down, instead of making the most of these holidays and my time with you. But suddenly I can't help thinking how awful it will be when the summer's over."

"Maybe it doesn't have to be," said Hannah.

"What do you mean?"

"Well," said Hannah, her expression thoughtful, "who's to say you can't go to my school and me to yours?"

"Oh, Hannah, how would I even get to yours from North Fitzroy?"

"I didn't mean it like that," Hannah said with a dismissive gesture. "I meant, you and I could swap places altogether, so that you'd live at my place in Armadale and I'd go live in North Fitzroy. Look, I know it's only been ten days, but so far we've fooled everyone. And if we can switch places for three weeks, why not for longer? In a few months' time, you might be brave enough to tell your mother how you really feel, and I might be a good-enough dancer to convince my parents that dancing's the real deal for me."

Simone was shaking her head, incredulous. "It's one thing getting away with it at summer school where they don't really know us, but at home? What chance have we got of fooling people who've known us all our lives?"

"We've got two things going for us," Hannah began. "Firstly, it will have been three weeks since they've seen us."

"So?"

"So they won't remember *exactly* what we look like."

"Why not? Are you expecting them to develop Alzheimer's while we're away?"

Hannah shot Simone a withering look. "No, of course not. But time makes you forget. For instance, my dad went overseas last year. He was only gone a couple of weeks, but sometimes I found it hard to remember his face. And when he came home again, I thought, *Oh, so THAT'S what he looks like*. It wasn't that I'd forgotten—I mean, I recognized him. But I'd forgotten little things, like the tiny scar on his jawline and the fact that one eyebrow is higher than the other."

"So, what you're saying is … "

"That memory isn't all that accurate. That's why we can get away with it, Sim. Sure, there are slight differences between us, but nothing anyone will notice after three whole weeks of not having seen us."

"Okay, maybe that's true … "

"And the second thing in our favor," said Hannah, "is that no one *knows* there are two of us—"

"We don't know that for sure," Simone interrupted.

"Well, chances are that no one knows, and if anyone did know, they'd have no reason to suspect that we know too. Think about it, Sim. Here, at Candance, we run the risk of being seen together, so we have to be *super* careful. But once we're back in Melbourne we'll be in different suburbs, different schools … "

Simone sighed. "I still don't see how we could pull it off. We don't know nearly enough about each other's lives."

"We've got ten more days together. That's ten long nights

and two more weekends. We can tell each other everything there is to know about each other's lives."

"Everything?"

"Well, all the important things. And once we're back in Melbourne, we can talk on the phone and meet up on Sundays. And if things get really desperate, we can always send an emergency text."

Simone shook her head. "Somehow, I doubt it would be that easy. I mean, what happens when your mum says something like, 'Remember the time you aced that science test? What was the trick question again?'"

"Sim," said Hannah, her expression grave, "I solemnly swear I have never, ever aced a science test."

Simone laughed, but suddenly Hannah was wrinkling her brow. "Actually, there is one thing I haven't thought of…" She drummed an unsteady rhythm on the tabletop. "Languages," she said at last. "What languages do you take at school?"

"French," said Simone. "You?"

"Well, that's the thing. I'm enrolled in Hebrew…"

*"Hebrew!"* Simone gave Hannah an I-told-you-so look. "You see?"

"No," said Hannah, shaking her head. "It'll be okay. I did French too, till the end of last year. And it's not too late for me—er, you—to drop Hebrew and switch back to French. Just make sure you go to the level convener's office on the first day of term."

Simone's jaw dropped open. "You say that as if we've definitely decided to go ahead with this…"

"Haven't we?"

"*No.*" Simone's voice was louder than she'd intended, and her cheeks flushed as other diners began to stare. "We're different," she continued, making sure to speak more softly. "We can't just change our whole identity. People will think we're being weird."

Hannah let out a burst of laughter. "We're allowed to be weird. We're moody teenagers, right? We can blame it on hormones."

"I guess so…" And at last Simone was laughing too. "God, I'll miss seeing you every day."

Hannah grinned. "So it's a deal? I'll go back to Melbourne as Simone Stark, and you'll go back as Hannah Segal?"

Simone hesitated, then shook her sister's outstretched hand. "Okay. Deal."

"Good," said Hannah. "Now lighten up and eat that pizza."

# eighteen

When Hannah rang her parents later that evening, she handed her iPhone straight to Simone. "You might as well start getting to know them. At least get used to the way they sound."

Simone stared at the phone as if unsure of what it was for.

"Speak," said Hannah.

"Um, hello?"

"Hannah, my love! How wonderful to hear from you!" The voice on the other end of the line was loud and deep, and Simone instinctively held the phone away from her ear.

She found herself smiling. "Uh, thanks ... Dad."

Hannah gave her a thumbs-up in silent approval.

"How's life treating my darling daughter?"

"Great," said Simone. "I'm having a fabulous time."

"Making friends?"

"Yes," she said, looking straight at Hannah as she spoke. "One very good one in particular."

"Excellent," said Manfred. "Well, we're thinking of you

all the time. We're counting the days... I'm handing the phone to Mum now."

And then Vanessa came on the line. "Everything all right? Enjoying Candance? I bumped into Dani earlier today." Dani, Simone already knew, was Hannah's best friend. "She said she misses you—you're never on Facebook, and your phone is almost never switched on."

"I've been busy," said Simone.

"I know. That's what I told her." Vanessa chatted on a little longer, mostly about people Simone had never heard of, and Simone said "Um" and "Yes" and "Uh-huh," and then the phone call was over.

Then it was time for Simone to call home. Harriet asked about Simone's dance classes, and Hannah launched into a detailed account of what the classes were like, what the teachers were like, and what they were rehearsing for the Candance concert.

"Don't overdo it," Simone warned, "or you won't sound like me."

"Don't worry," Hannah whispered, covering the mouthpiece. "People always believe you when you tell them what they want to hear."

———————

Simone spent the following morning making lists of everything Hannah would need to know. And she drew maps— of her house, of North Fitzroy, of the VSD and how to get there. By the time Hannah came back from class, she had pages and pages ready to give her.

"Let's eat first," said Hannah, pulling off her leotard and shorts and dropping them straight on the floor. "What should I wear?" She yanked open the closet door, revealing the clothes she'd dumped inside. A couple of tops spilled off the shelf into an open drawer. "You choose," she said to Simone, "while I have a shower."

"It's a little hard to see," said Simone, following Hannah into the bathroom. "You do know, don't you, that my mother's a neat freak?"

"Uh, so you said."

"She'd have convulsions if she saw the state of your wardrobe."

"What can I do? I'm naturally messy," Hannah said. "She'll have to adjust."

"No way," said Simone. "But don't worry, I'll show you how to keep your closets tidy. I've got a foolproof system."

"A system?"

"You need a system when my mum's around. See, she has a certain way of sorting clothes, and a certain way of folding them. And she gets really anxious if you fold something that should be hung, or hang something that should be folded."

"Yikes! Scary!" Hannah drew the shower curtain behind her and turned on the taps. The rush of water put a temporary end to the conversation, but it continued two hours later over a Mexican dinner of enchiladas topped with cheese.

"Always remember to close the lid of the toilet seat," Simone was saying. "She hates it left up."

"You're joking, right?"

"Sadly, no." Simone consulted the neatly written list she'd brought along. "Never leave anything out on the bathroom sink. Never leave lids off jars, and never squeeze the toothpaste from the middle of the tube."

"Where do I squeeze it from?" asked Hannah, puzzled.

"The bottom, of course, and work your way up."

Hannah sighed. "So many rules!"

"You get used to it. Now tell me something *I* need to know."

"Things are pretty laid-back at my house," Hannah said.

"I thought Jews had rules about food?"

"They do, in theory," Hannah said, "but we're not religious, so we don't keep kosher. Though we don't eat pig."

"What if my mum makes pork for dinner?" asked Simone.

"Um ... I'll tell her I've become vegetarian?"

Simone shook her head. "No, don't do that. She wouldn't cope. Just say you've gone off pig, and that you can't stand the smell of it cooking in the kitchen. And speaking of kitchens ..." Simone once again consulted her list. "Never leave dishes on the counter or in the sink. They have to go straight into the dishwasher. And if the dishwasher's full, make sure you empty it without being asked. Oh, and ... why aren't you writing all of this down?"

Hannah shrugged. "You already have."

———

Sam had scored four free tickets for a matinee performance of Bangarra Dance Theatre, and on Sunday morning she came to Simone's room with Tom and Liam and knocked on the door.

"Simone, are you ready?"

Hannah pushed Simone toward the door and hid in the bathroom while Simone opened the door a crack and poked her head out. "I'm really sorry, but I've got a headache. You guys will have to go without me."

"Poor Simone," said Sam. "Will you be okay?"

Simone faked a tired but courageous smile. "Yeah, it's just that Bangarra dances to loud drumming and I don't think I can face that sort of noise right now."

"Fair enough," said Sam.

Sam and Liam headed off, but Tom lingered. "I could stay and keep you company? Massage your head?" He took a step closer and once again Simone had that tingly feeling even though they weren't actually touching. He'd just had a shower, and he smelled of soap and shampoo. Now she really was beginning to feel lightheaded.

"Th … thanks," she stammered, feeling her face flush red, "but I have to lie down."

He chuckled softly. "Is that supposed to put me off?" He brushed a wisp of hair off her forehead and Simone shivered. "You know, you really are different when you're on your own."

Simone swallowed and didn't answer.

"So, can I stay?"

"Sorry," she murmured, with an almost imperceptible shake of her head.

Disappointment flickered in his eyes before he lowered them and backed away.

"Wait!" she said.

He looked up, his expression carefully guarded.

"Could you wait just a second?" Simone dashed into the room and came back with a pen. "Can I borrow your arm?"

He held out his arm, which was smooth and finely muscled and golden tan.

From his elbow to his wrist, she scrawled her mobile number in large, wobbly digits, hoping he wouldn't notice that her hand was shaking.

"What's this?" he asked.

"My phone number. In case you want to call me when we're back in Melbourne."

He flashed her a grin. "I will," he said.

"You'd better hurry before the others leave without you. Enjoy Bangarra."

"I'd enjoy it more if you were coming. Take care of that head."

———

"That was dumb," Simone said to Hannah after he'd gone. "I gave him my phone number."

"Why was that dumb?"

"Because if we're swapping lives, we'll have to swap phones."

Hannah continued brushing her hair. "Don't worry. I like arranging dates on your behalf. I'll let you know when he calls." She twisted her hair into a knot at the top of her head. "You know, you should have gone with them, or spent the day with Tom."

"You know I couldn't. We have to get our hair trimmed today, and I promised I'd go with you when you got your ears pierced."

"Why? Will it hurt?"

"A bit," said Simone, "but not for long."

Two hours later, they came out of the salon and made their way to the pharmacy—their shiny-clean, newly cut hair falling in identical waves to just below their shoulders. They grinned at their reflections in the pharmacy's windows.

"I can't remember now," said Hannah, "if I'm me or you."

"Now *that's* scary," said Simone, pushing Hannah inside.

Hannah clutched her sister's arm as soon as the stud gun came into view.

"Relax," said the pharmacist, swiping her earlobe with alcohol. "It's not like I haven't done this before."

Simone looked on sympathetically and Hannah gritted her teeth.

"I'll count to three," said the pharmacist. "One. Two—"

"*Eiooooww!*" Hannah's shriek pierced the air. "Bloody hell, Sim, that was torture."

"If it's any consolation, I'm pretty sure you've bruised my arm."

Out in the street again, Hannah was swearing and Simone was rubbing her arm.

Simone laughed. "I bet you burst that poor man's eardrum."

"Thanks for the sympathy. My ears are throbbing."

"They'll be fine. Clean them daily, give the studs a twist every now and then, and wear nothing but gold for at least two months."

"Yes, Mum," said Hannah.

The two girls giggled at the word "Mum," then gazed into each other's eyes.

"I wonder what she was like," said Hannah after a while.

"She was probably a cross between you and me. I wish I'd known her. And our dad."

"Me too," said Hannah, "but at least we're getting to know each other."

"Yeah, which reminds me, you'd better tell me more about your friends at Carmel College. And all your teachers…"

"Right," said Hannah. "And you'll need to know who everyone is at Armadale Dance."

"So I'll still be doing dance classes?" Simone asked.

"I think you'd better. My parents would get really suspicious if you suddenly wanted to give up dancing. But it'll only be three times a week—it won't be like dancing at the VSD."

# nineteen

The last day of Candance had arrived, and though classes weren't normally held on a Sunday, today was an exception, since the concert was scheduled for two o'clock. Morning class and rehearsal were over, and the dancers had been sent to their rooms to rest. Hannah, too excited to do anything as mundane as lie in bed, had not stopped talking.

Now she was preparing for the performance. She slid a final hairpin into her bun and slipped a hairnet on top. Then she grabbed a bottle of hair spray, closed her eyes, and pressed the trigger. "Wish me luck," she said to Simone.

"You don't need it. You'll be brilliant." Simone tossed her the pointe shoes. "Hey, don't forget these."

"Your lucky pointe shoes," Hannah said.

"*Our* lucky pointe shoes," Simone corrected. "I wish I could come and watch you dancing."

"So do I." Hannah blew Simone a kiss and shut the door.

When the sound of her footsteps had receded, it seemed to Simone that all the courage she'd gained from her spirited twin had departed with her. Alone in the room, she thought about the plans they'd made. In just a few hours she'd be on her way to Melbourne, and to Hannah's life, and the truth was she had no idea just what that life was really like.

Swapping lives with Hannah might be a good idea in theory, but with the reality imminent, it seemed like a drastic solution to their problems. The fact was, she would be living in a house full of strangers, and Hannah wouldn't be there to shore her up when the going got tough and make her laugh when she slipped up.

Simone wondered how she'd ever let Hannah talk her into it.

———

She was still brooding two hours later when Hannah came bouncing into the room, her face flushed with happiness.

"How did it go?"

"It was fabulous, Sim. God, I love performing. I can't wait to start dancing at the VSD."

"Aren't you even a *tiny* bit worried you might miss your old life?"

"Worried? No."

"You're *really* sure you want to do this?"

"Of course," said Hannah. "Why, aren't you?"

Simone didn't answer at first. She opened her mouth, then closed it again, her lips twisting as she tried to formulate her thoughts. "Not as sure as you," she said at last.

"Just remember our pact," said Hannah firmly. "As soon

as one of us wants to swap back, the other agrees. No arguments. No discussion."

"Right," said Simone. "And we'll ring each other."

"Absolutely. Every night when we're in bed."

Simone nodded. "Okay then. Come on, we'd better pack." She opened the wardrobe and pulled out her dull, mustard-colored suitcase.

"You've got a vomit-colored suitcase," Hannah said.

Simone laughed. "My mum bought it the year I first came to Candance."

"Hmm!" Hannah retrieved her own bright red suitcase from beneath the bed. "We'd better swap," she said, pushing the case with the shiny plastic shell toward Simone. "I'll pack your suitcase; you pack mine."

Simone shook her head. "We have to go home with the same clothes we left with, so we should pack our own and swap when we've finished." She was already transferring neat piles of shorts and T-shirts into her suitcase, which now lay open on her bed.

Hannah tossed her own clothes onto the bed opposite, then made a half-hearted attempt to fold them.

Simone frowned. "I thought I showed you how to fold clothes."

"Don't worry, Sim. This suitcase is going back to my place, remember? I don't need to be tidy till I get to your house. Hey, listen…"

Ripples of laughter and bursts of conversation echoed through the hallway. Above the din in the corridor, the voices of Liam, Sam, and Tom could be heard.

"They're high on adrenaline, like me," said Hannah. "Post-performance euphoria."

"You know what that is, don't you?" said Simone. "Relief that you made it through alive."

"Could be," said Hannah, grinning. "Shhh..." she cautioned. The voices out in the corridor grew louder and nearer. Then came a drumbeat on the door.

"I'll nick into the bathroom," Simone whispered, "while you say goodbye."

"Shouldn't you be the one to say goodbye? Don't you want to see Tom?"

Simone quickly shook her head. "I don't have your performance afterglow, or any leftover makeup..."

"You're right," said Hannah. She stepped out into the corridor to say farewell to her friends.

Sam draped an arm across her shoulder. "I'll miss you, Simone. Liam and I have decided to visit Melbourne over the Easter holidays."

"Really? That'll be great."

Now Liam stepped in for a hug. "It was a fantastic summer."

"My turn," said Tom, pulling Hannah tight against him. "I wish we had time for a proper goodbye."

Liam groaned. "Cut the drama. You'll see each other. You both live in Melbourne. Come on, mate. You've got a plane to catch."

# twenty

Candance was over. It was getting dark, and most of the staff and students had already left. The few who remained were nowhere in sight, and the campus that had been buzzing with noise and excitement just a few hours before was now deserted. A sense of anticlimax hung in the air, adding a tinge of sadness to the silence.

The two girls stood outside the main entrance to the campus, waiting for the taxi that would take them to the airport. Hannah would board Simone's eight o'clock flight, and Simone would leave on Hannah's flight an hour later.

As the taxi came into view, Simone shivered, though not from cold. "I still can't believe we're doing this," she said again.

"It is a bit scary," Hannah admitted. "But what's the worst that could happen? I mean, none of our parents are axe murderers, so how bad could it be?"

Simone managed a weak half-smile but didn't answer.

Hannah placed a hand on her sister's arm. "We don't have

to do this if it's not what you want. You can still change your mind."

Simone hesitated. To any sane person, their plan would surely seem irrational. Should she call the whole thing off? But then she'd have to return to the VSD, and she couldn't go back there. Not now. Not yet. Perhaps not ever.

Besides, in spite of her doubts, she had to admit she'd been looking forward to an inside view of Hannah's life. But for the luck of the draw, Hannah's life might have been her own, and this was a once-in-a-lifetime opportunity. How many people could literally change places with somebody else?

She glanced at Hannah, who looked worried that she might actually change her mind. "It's okay," Simone said softly, reaching out to touch her shoulder. "Let's stick to our plan."

The taxi pulled up, the driver loaded the luggage into the trunk, and the girls climbed wordlessly into the back of the car. They clasped hands all the way to the airport as the taxi sped silently through the warm Canberra night.

After Hannah checked in, they sat at a table in a small airport café and sipped cappuccinos as once again they went over the important details of each other's lives.

Then it was time. Time for goodbyes. Time for Hannah to board the plane.

The girls flung their arms around each other for one final embrace.

A moment later, Hannah was gone and Simone was alone. She wheeled Hannah's suitcase to the Qantas check-in. And there was nothing else to do but lift the suitcase onto the conveyor belt and collect her boarding pass, because now it really was too late to change her mind.

———————

On board flight QF483, Hannah was too excited to mind being trapped between an elderly lady wearing cloying perfume and a middle-aged man with horrid BO. Candance had been the best experience of her life, and it was just the beginning. Had she been going straight home to her old life, right now she'd be trying to stifle her disappointment that Candance had ended. The high of performing was always followed by a sense of anticlimax that lasted for days. This time, there was no chance of that. She was about to embark on a whole new adventure.

She thought with affection of her family back home and wondered whether she would have behaved any differently, the last time she saw them, if she'd known that she wouldn't be sure when she'd see them again.

At Candance, with a full schedule of classes and every spare minute spent with Simone, there'd been no time to miss the family and friends who'd been such an important part of her life. Now, alone on the plane, she experienced a pang of nostalgia. But if Hannah had any reservations about what she was doing, she did not want to admit them, even to herself. That would be a sign of weakness.

She'd loved every moment of the summer school, and knew she'd developed as a dancer. Now she was ready—ready to fool the staff at the VSD into thinking she was in fact the very accomplished Simone. If she could pull it off, she would have earned her place there. And when her parents finally knew the truth, they would have to believe she'd been born to dance.

The elderly lady with the cloying perfume had fallen asleep, her head bouncing gently up and down on Hannah's shoulder, and the man with the horrid BO was drinking beer, so that bad breath combined with BO wafted her way. But Hannah would put up with far worse if it meant she could dance at the VSD.

The plane touched down at Melbourne Airport. Hannah was jittery. She wished the queue to the exit would move faster because she couldn't wait to disembark.

The airport was crowded, and some of the passengers who'd been on her flight were in the midst of emotional reunions with family or friends. There were a number of middle-aged women who more or less fit the description of Simone's mum, and Hannah wondered which of them was Harriet. Simone hadn't been able to show her any photos of her mum—she didn't have any in her Facebook albums, and Harriet wasn't on Facebook herself.

"How will I recognize her?" Hannah had asked. "What if I can't figure out which one she is?"

"You won't have a problem," Simone had assured her. "She'll be the one calling my name so loudly that everyone will think you're deaf."

"Simone! Simone!" A woman in a pale blue, short-sleeved dress buttoned to the collar was waving a hand above the crowd as she hurried toward her, and even when Hannah acknowledged her wave, she continued calling, "Simone! Simone!"

Hannah smiled to herself. Simone's description had been spot-on. Not one to shy away from attention, she let out a yell to rival Harriet's. "Hi, Mum! I'm over here." The word "mum" in this context sounded strange, and the moment it left her lips, Hannah felt as if she'd betrayed Vanessa.

But there was no time for regrets, for Harriet was moving quickly toward her. She clasped Hannah briefly, pecked her cheek, and stepped away. "Come on then, we'd better go."

That was it? That was the grand reunion? Hannah couldn't help feeling a little let down.

"Now, tell me all about Candance," Simone's mum began.

---

Simone sat in her assigned seat by the window and gazed out into the darkness, contemplating what lay ahead.

She had left Melbourne as Simone and would return as Hannah. To that end, she would have to adopt some of Hannah's passion and resolve. How could she be more like her identical twin? She thought of the acting classes she'd taken at school. "It's not enough," one teacher had said, "to *act* the character. You must *become* the character."

Simone had spent three weeks with Hannah and had come to know her. They were so similar in some ways, and so different in others ... Above all, Hannah was outgoing, friendly, and fearless. *What does that feel like?* Simone wondered. *Can I access those qualities? Are they buried inside me? Do they belong to a person I might still become?*

She visualized herself behaving like Hannah, but when the plane landed and she followed the other passengers into an airport swarming with people, somehow she was just Simone —shy, reserved, and incredibly nervous. Trying to calm herself, she took a deep breath and looked around.

"Hannah, my love!" The booming voice could be easily heard above the crowd.

Simone looked up to see a large, jolly-looking man striding toward her, and a moment later she was enveloped in an enormous bear hug.

Simone had seen photos of Hannah's dad, but they hadn't prepared her for the actual size of him. It took her a moment before she had the presence of mind to hug him back. She hadn't guessed quite how enormous he'd be and how small she'd feel when crushed against his massive chest. He was like a friendly giant, with balding hair, a dark bushy beard, and thick-rimmed glasses. His larger-than-life presence was a shock, and Simone hoped he couldn't feel her body trembling. As she stood in his arms, the powerful scent of aftershave—or was it cologne?—assailed her nostrils.

"And what about a hug for me?" said the smiling woman by his side. This must be Vanessa, Hannah's mum. She was slight and well-groomed, with light, inquiring eyes, and she wore a touch of some pleasant perfume.

Simone embraced her tentatively while Vanessa held her tightly and then stepped back, holding both Simone's hands in her own. "You look wonderful, darling. Manfred, doesn't she look wonderful?"

And somehow they'd reached the baggage claim—though Simone couldn't remember actually moving—and Manfred was plucking Hannah's suitcase off the conveyor belt as if it were no heavier than a handbag. Then the three of them were walking toward the exit, and it wasn't long before Hannah's suitcase had been placed in the trunk of a navy BMW, and Simone was sitting comfortably in the back seat with the familiar lights of Melbourne flashing by.

# twenty-one

From the street, the house looked tiny. Intermittent street-lights cast a glow that gave just enough light to distinguish one dwelling from the next. Simone's was one in a row of identical homes. Their front doors were only a couple of meters from the road. There were no large boulevard strips or sprawling front lawns, and no carports or garages. Harriet parked a little way down the street, and Hannah lugged Simone's suitcase along the footpath and up two steps to the Starks' front door.

"Pop the suitcase in your room, Simone, and come and have a cup of tea."

Hannah made her way along the narrow hallway, sniffing at the strange, cabbage-like odor that suffused the air. Strange how you could describe a home in detail, as Simone had—the exact location and number of rooms—yet fail to capture its very essence, which was indefinable and had something to do with smell, and atmosphere, and age.

Simone's room was the second door on the left. It was as neat as Hannah had imagined it would be, and very small, with cream-painted walls and wooden floorboards covered by a pastel rug. There was a desk, a chair, and two small shelves. One shelf housed a small collection of books. The other was home to a few ornaments and a couple of photos.

Hannah put the suitcase down and went to take a closer look. The photos showed Simone with friends. Hannah could have sworn the snapshots were of herself—except they couldn't be, as she didn't know the other people in them, and Simone was wearing clothes that Hannah didn't own and had never worn.

Simone's bed was immaculately made up with a pretty set of floral sheets. A small stuffed teddy bear lay on the pillow, and on the wall above the bed was a poster of two ballet stars dancing a pas-de-deux. It was signed, *To Simone, love Mum.*

Hannah now hoisted the suitcase onto the bed and flung it open, then wandered over to the wardrobe, which was small and painted cream to match the walls. Inside, the clothes were perfectly folded. Hannah sighed. She'd never match this standard of neatness.

Suddenly, Hannah missed Simone with an intensity she'd rarely felt before, and the thought of sleeping in her room was strangely comforting. It was the next best thing to being with her.

"Simone!" Harriet's call interrupted her thoughts. "I've made your tea."

Hannah left the unpacking and went to join Simone's mum in the old-fashioned kitchen.

"You're looking well," Harriet said. "Something's different —have you cut your hair?"

"Yeah, just a trim. What do you think?"

"Nice, said Harriet. "You know my rule—if it's long enough to make a bun, it's fine by me. Now, drink your tea before it gets cold."

"Thanks," said Hannah, as Harriet indicated the mug on the kitchen table. She took a sip and put the cup down.

"What's wrong?"

"Uh…nothing. Just, it's a little bitter. Could I have sugar?"

"Sugar!" Harriet exclaimed, as if Hannah had requested poison. "Since when do you take sugar?"

"That's how they served the tea at Candance. I'm used to it now."

"You know we don't keep sugar in this house."

Hannah frowned. "Could we buy some?"

"Buy some? You're a dancer, Simone. Sugar's the last thing you need. You know what I think about wasted calories. And you've always had such good eating habits. Don't start developing bad ones now."

Hannah could think of several things she might have said in reply: *Shouldn't that be up to me to? Why do YOU care what goes into my mouth? You can't control every aspect of my life.*

But she didn't want to get on the wrong side of Harriet on the very first day. And if Simone had to put up with Harriet's rules, it was only fair that she did too.

Lying in Simone's bed a little later, Hannah tried to imagine what it would have been like living her whole life with a woman as controlling as Harriet Stark. It wasn't just that Harriet tried to micro-manage her daughter's life. It was more that she lacked…what was it? Warmth, perhaps? Harriet hadn't even asked if she was hungry—unlike her own mum, who would have offered her a sandwich, or chocolate cake, or scones with cream.

Hannah thought longingly of her family at home. They might be only a twenty-minute drive away, but they might as well have been in another country.

Suddenly, she felt very alone. Up until yesterday she'd had a proper family: two parents, a brother, a dog, and even— most recently—a wonderful sister. Now she had only a domineering and highly strung woman for company.

Still, the day after tomorrow, she'd begin her training at the VSD...

The sound of a Chopin concerto filtered under her door, with Harriet humming along. Hannah snuggled deeper under the covers, and as she waited for Simone to call, she imagined performing a beautiful *adage*, her arms soft, her extensions magnificent, her back erect and statuesque.

# twenty-two

It was almost midnight when the car turned into the driveway of Hannah's sprawling Armadale home. A single lamp lit up the entrance to the front door, but they drove past it and entered the house through a door off the garage. A large, barking Labrador jumped up and slobbered all over Simone, sending her toppling into Manfred.

"Kimmy missed you," said Vanessa, laughing. "He was such a misery bag after you left."

"Calm down, boy," Manfred boomed cheerfully, "or you'll knock her over."

Simone reached out a tentative hand to pat the animal. Then, realizing that Hannah would probably match the canine's greeting with equal fervor, she put both arms around him and ruffled his fur.

When the dog had settled down, Simone saw she was in an open kitchen that spilled into a large and comfortable living room. Despite the barking, laughing, raised voices, TV blaring, and door slamming, Hannah's brother Adam was asleep on the couch.

Following her gaze, Vanessa said, "He was determined to wait up for you. I just knew he wouldn't last—not after riding his bike and swimming all day." Her expression was soft, her voice filled with affection. Then she turned her attention back to Simone, who was still surveying her surroundings, taking in the size of the room and the fact that it was warm and welcoming. "Home always looks different when you've been away."

"It does," Simone agreed.

"When things are too familiar you just stop seeing them, but time away makes you open your eyes."

Simone gave Vanessa a wistful smile.

"So, how was Candance?"

"Uh … great!" said Simone.

"You haven't said a word about it, and I thought you'd be talking our ears off."

Simone chuckled. She could just imagine Hannah talking their ears off.

"Are you hungry, darling? Did you eat on the plane?"

Simone shook her head. Now that Vanessa had brought her attention to the subject of food, she realized that the pleasant aroma she'd noticed before was in fact the smell of freshly baked cake.

"No you're not hungry, or no you didn't eat on the plane?"

"Both," said Simone.

"I spent the afternoon baking. You've got a choice between poppy-seed swirl, orange cake, and pecan pie."

Simone shook her head. "Thanks, but…maybe tomorrow."

"No to cake? You must be even more exhausted than you look. Why don't you go up to bed?"

Simone nodded, then mumbled good night. Manfred picked up Hannah's suitcase and crossed the kitchen in just a few strides. Half in a daze, Simone followed him down a hallway, up a flight of stairs, and into Hannah's room. He put the suitcase down with a flourish and a "There you are, Ma'am," and once again Simone was enfolded in this giant's embrace.

And then Manfred was gone, leaving behind his lingering scent. Simone was alone in Hannah's room.

It was about three times the size of her room at home, and far more luxurious. Wall-to-wall-carpet—the same rich green carpet that lined the staircase and the upstairs hall—covered the floor, and the walls were painted lemon and white. The curtains too were lemon and white, with a delicate pattern of tiny green leaves. Five shelves and a massive desk took up almost an entire wall. One shelf housed textbooks, including some French ones. There were also a few books in a language Simone didn't recognize. Possibly Hebrew. A couple of those seemed to come with translations. She pulled one out and looked at it. The English title on the front said *The Jewish Book of Prayer*. The foreign language title was on the back, except that the front seemed to be where the book ended, and vice versa.

She put it back and looked at the books on the other shelves. Most were novels, and many bore the imprint of Seagull Press. Simone ran a hand along their spines, avoiding the temptation to read their titles or she'd be up all night. She sat down for a moment at Hannah's desk, which was covered in knickknacks, photos, and souvenirs. Not for the first time, she wished she'd shared her sister's life.

Pushing that thought aside, she began to unpack. Hannah's wardrobe was in a state of chaos. Simone emptied all the drawers and closets, then folded each item individually. Half an hour later, the wardrobe bore a passing resemblance to her wardrobe at home, and Simone felt a little calmer.

She showered in Hannah's ensuite bathroom and put on Hannah's baby doll pajamas, which were crumpled but clean. Then she slipped into Hannah's bed, which was bigger and more comfortable than the one she was used to. The lacy white quilt cover, with its pink satin trimming, had a matching pillowcase, and Simone thought they were very pretty. She rested her head on the plumped up pillow, clutching Hannah's iPhone.

A handsome Hollywood actor smiled down at her from posters on the wall above. Suddenly Simone was hungry and wished she had accepted a slice of cake. She wouldn't go downstairs and ask—not when she'd have to confront Vanessa and Manfred again. Not that Hannah's parents hadn't been wonderful. It was just that keeping up the pretence was a strain, and now she needed some time alone.

A little while later, footsteps and murmured voices passed her door. Manfred and Vanessa were going to bed. Soon the strip of light under her door went dark.

At last, the house was completely quiet, and when Simone

was sure that everyone had gone to sleep, she rang the familiar number of her own mobile phone.

"Sim! How are you? I've been waiting ages for your call."

And although it had only been a few hours since she'd last seen Hannah, Simone almost cried because it felt so good to hear her voice.

# twenty-three

Hannah opened the bedroom door and peered along the narrow hallway, wondering whether Harriet was already up. The bathroom door creaked open and Hannah withdrew into the bedroom just as Harriet emerged. She held her breath and listened, waiting till the sound of footsteps passed her door. Then she grabbed a pair of Simone's shorts and a T-shirt and hurried into the bathroom to shower and change, not yet comfortable enough in her new surroundings to laze around in her pajamas until after breakfast, as she would have at home.

By the time she entered the kitchen, Harriet had gone to work. She'd left a note on the kitchen table: *Back by six. Call if you need anything. Love, Mum.*

Perfect. Hannah could explore the house and neighborhood openly, with no interruptions. As she hadn't eaten anything since leaving Canberra the night before, she'd start with the kitchen.

Dishes were stacked neatly in the kitchen cupboards,

along with glasses and mugs, pots and pans. Cutlery was in the top drawer under the sink, and food was in a cupboard beside the fridge—two boxes of cereal and one of oats, a few tins of tuna and sardines, two cans of baked beans, a tin of rice cakes, one unopened jar of pickles, a box of tea bags, and a jar half-full of instant coffee. Next to the microwave was a bread bin, containing a single loaf of whole-grain bread.

The closest thing to sugar was a pot of honey. There were no cookies or cake, and no flour for baking. Hannah opened the fridge, hoping its contents would be generous enough to make up for the lack of a decent pantry, but it held nothing but a carton of milk, a half-finished container of cottage cheese, plain yogurt, six eggs, and half a melon.

There was something frugal—stingy, even—about this kitchen, Hannah concluded, remembering the well-stocked pantry at home. She let out a small sigh of resignation and helped herself to a serving of Sultana Bran and a slice of melon, then washed her dishes, returned the kitchen to the immaculate state in which she'd found it, and wandered over to the living room.

She hadn't seen this room before. In contrast to the kitchen—with its sparse furnishings and nothing but a rather ordinary calendar hanging on the wall—this room, though small, was densely furnished, with comfortable couches in muted florals on a thick cream carpet. But what really caught Hannah's attention were the magnificent photos, which covered almost every available inch of wall space. All were of Simone in full dance costume, mostly in some sort of dance pose—an *arabesque*, an *attitude en pointe*, a *relevé* with her arms in fifth, a *grand jeté* in which she seemed to be flying.

*That could be me,* Hannah thought as she studied a particularly beautiful photo of Simone leaping through the air, legs stretched and toes pointed, arms soft and head erect. *They could all be me.*

In fact, if she hadn't known better, Hannah might have thought they were her. She felt a pang of envy, and wished she could believe that she too were capable of such perfection.

In some of the photos, Simone looked as if she were about to go onstage, or had just finished a performance. In every one of them, her face was made up, her hair was immaculate, and she was artfully positioned for the camera.

The photos spanned several years. There were older ones, taken when Simone was five, six, seven years old—a cute Simone in tap shoes, a mini-skirt, and missing teeth—and later ones, when she was perhaps nine, ten, eleven years old. In many of them, Simone held a trophy of some sort, or wore a medal around her neck. In the photos taken in recent years, Simone held nothing but the occasional bouquet of flowers. The trophies must have stopped when she'd started training at the VSD, where students weren't allowed to compete.

Hannah circled the room again, taking a closer look at each photo in turn. The more she looked, the more it seemed that something was wrong with the overall picture. At first she couldn't work out what it was. But the realization gradually grew on her ... there wasn't a single photo of the real Simone. No snapshots of birthday parties, Christmas parties, family gatherings. No photos of her at the zoo, in the country, on a mountain, at the beach. The entire room was like a shrine to dance—with no sign of Simone having a life apart from dancing. Talk about having ballet shoved down your throat!

Hannah was beginning to understand a little of what Simone's life must have been like. Suddenly, she was overcome by an overwhelming sadness for her twin.

She made her way to Harriet's bedroom and paused. Then, with a stab of guilt, she opened the door, hoping to find photos of Simone astride a horse, on a bike, stuffing chocolate cake into her mouth, or yelling as she rode the Ferris wheel at Luna Park.

Harriet's room was as neat and tidy as the rest of the house, with a double bed in the center, a couple of Renoir prints on the walls, and two photos on the dressing table. One was of Simone as a baby. The other was of a much younger Harriet with a good-looking man. They had their arms around each other and even though they were looking into the camera and not at each other, you could tell they were happy. This must be the fiancé who had died.

Hannah opened Harriet's wardrobe, revealing clothes folded so professionally they could have appeared in an ad for *Home Beautiful*. The closet next to it contained nothing but costumes—possibly every costume Simone had ever worn—that hung in order from biggest to smallest. Next to them was a set of drawers... which might contain the kinds of photos she was looking for.

Hannah hesitated. It was bad enough entering Harriet's room. Did she really have the right to rifle through her personal belongings?

The phone rang and Hannah jumped. She closed the closet doors and ran to the kitchen to answer the call.

"Simone, I'm glad I caught you," Harriet said. "I forgot to tell you the washing machine was fixed last week, so you can do your laundry."

Hannah stared at the phone, too stunned to speak.

"Simone, can you hear me? Are you there?"

"Yes, but—"

"Sorry, got to go. Just thought I should let you know so you won't have to lug your stuff to the Laundromat. You'd better get the washing done today, what with school starting tomorrow. See you tonight, then."

The line went dead, and Hannah was still staring at the mouthpiece. Had she misheard? Or did Harriet actually expect her to do her own laundry? Hannah had never used a washing machine before. Her mum had always done laundry for her.

A scene from the movie *Just My Luck* popped into her head: Lindsay Lohan trying to work the washing machine, flooding the room with soap and bubbles, losing her footing on the slippery floor and practically drowning...

Hannah buried her face in her hands, wishing she hadn't answered the phone, but it was too late now. She took a deep breath and tried to stem her rising panic. She'd call Simone and ask for instructions. How hard could it be?

# twenty-four

Even after speaking to Hannah on the phone, Simone had lain in bed in a mild state of anxiety, and it was hours before she'd fallen asleep. She woke to the sound of voices calling—or was it a radio blaring? It was a little after nine o'clock.

She opened the curtains. Below her was a garden, and next to it a patio with a white fiberglass table and six matching chairs. The sky was very blue and clear. Simone opened a window and a warm breeze wafted in.

It was Monday, she remembered, the only day she had to familiarize herself with her new surroundings before the school year began. She dressed quickly before heading downstairs.

Vanessa was in the kitchen making pancakes, and Adam was sitting at the table, tucking in. His face lit up when he saw her. "Hey, sis!" he said with a grin.

"Hey, Adam!"

Kimmy bounded over to Simone with a joyful bark, springing up to lick her cheek.

"That dog spent a whole week moping after you left," Vanessa said. "I can't say I blame him. All of us missed you."

Simone glanced shyly at Hannah's mum. "I missed you, too."

"How many pancakes, sweetie?" asked Vanessa. "One or two?"

"Just one to start with," said Simone.

Vanessa slid one large pancake onto a dinner plate and set it down in front of Simone, then brought her own plate over and sat down to join her.

"So," said Vanessa, "tell me all about Candance. I know you're dying to."

"Uh…"

"What were the other dancers like? Meet anyone interesting?"

Simone doused the pancake with maple syrup. "Yeah. The other dancers were really friendly." She tossed her hair back over her shoulders, and suddenly Vanessa was staring at her ears.

"What?" said Simone, beginning to panic.

"You got your ears pierced," said Vanessa. "We agreed that you wouldn't. Not until you turned eighteen."

Simone put a forkful of pancake into her mouth and chewed slowly, stalling for time. She wasn't sure how she'd explain the pierced ears, even though Hannah had warned her that Manfred and Vanessa would disapprove.

"*You* agreed," she said at last, in what she hoped was Hannah's carefree tone. "I never promised."

"But—"

"You were worried my ears would get infected, right? But look, I'm fine."

"Your father thinks it's mutilation . . ." Vanessa began, but the telephone rang and she went to answer it.

"Good one, Hannah," Adam said, giving her a thumbs-up with a devilish smile.

Simone stuck her tongue out at him as she'd seen Hannah do in one of her photos. Then they were making faces at each other, and laughing, and it occurred to Simone that having a younger brother might be fun.

When she'd finished eating, she put her plate in the sink, and while Adam tucked into another pancake, Simone went to explore.

The house seemed different in the light of day. Large windows looked out onto the same well-tended and luscious garden she'd seen from her room. And inside, the furnishings were cozy and inviting, the colors around her rich and warm. There was a spacious lounge-dining room off the kitchen-family room, and beyond that a large study in which stood two desks—one each for Manfred and Vanessa?—as well as a TV and stereo system. But what drew her the most were the three walls lined, floor to ceiling, with bookshelves, all of which were full of books stacked tightly together.

Simone had never seen so many books in a private home. She stood for a moment, admiring them, before heading upstairs, where she poked her head into each of the bedrooms—Manfred and Vanessa's, Adam's, and one she supposed was a guest room. Another door off the upstairs hallway led to a bathroom, where Adam had left dirty clothes and a sopping towel on the tiled floor.

Resisting the distinctly un-Hannahlike impulse to tidy up, and grateful that she didn't have to share a bathroom with him, Simone returned to Hannah's room and grabbed Hannah's bag before heading downstairs.

"If she asks," she said to Adam, not quite able to call Vanessa "Mum," "tell her I've gone for a walk."

"Okay," said Adam.

As the front door closed behind her, Simone felt herself relax. It was a relief to be outside and on her own.

---

She found herself in a curving, tree-lined street where large old trees rose majestically from generous boulevard strips and dipped their heads to form a canopy over the road. The houses—built in a mix of styles, some old, some new—were huge compared to those she was used to, and now and again she passed a grand and sweeping mansion. In between the larger streets ran short, narrow ones, devoid of boulevard strips. Here were rows of shoe-box homes, as small as those in North Fitzroy and not unlike them.

Simone was still exploring the neighborhood when Hannah phoned.

"Sim, you've got to help me."

After Simone had calmed her down and talked her through the process of doing the laundry, she apologized for about the twentieth time. "I'm sorry I didn't mention it," she told Hannah, "but how should I know you'd never done a load of laundry? By the way," she added, "your mum noticed my pierced ears. She wasn't pleased."

"I warned you," said Hannah.

"Do you think she'll still be mad when I get home?"

"I doubt it," said Hannah. "My parents are good like that. They might get mad for a minute, but they let things go."

# twenty-five

*It's make my own or starve*, thought Hannah, as Harriet left for work without first preparing the kind of packed lunch that she was used to. Luckily, Hannah was up early and had plenty of time. What's more, Harriet had been to the market the day before and returned with a small but excellent choice of fruit and vegetables.

Hannah made herself a cheese and lettuce sandwich and packed it in a thermal bag along with some freshly cut carrot sticks, a nectarine, and a bunch of grapes. Then she let herself out of the silent house. Following Simone's directions, she turned left, crossed Edinburgh Gardens, and boarded the number 86 tram. Her heart was racing, and she barely registered the unfamiliar streetscape sliding by.

The VSD was a ten-minute walk from Flinders Street Station, and, compared to Carmel College, it was tiny. The school was comprised of three or four buildings, with covered walkways in between and a single courtyard. Hannah had arrived with twenty minutes to spare, in which she intended to familiarize herself with her new surroundings.

"Good morning, Simone!"

Hannah spun around. Two people were walking toward her. One was a pleasant-looking man with a neat moustache —no doubt Mr. Collins, the school principal; the other was a redhaired girl about her own age who seemed excited but apprehensive, much like Hannah herself.

"How are you today?" the principal asked.

"Fine, thank you, Mr. Collins," Hannah said.

"I'm glad I caught you. This is Julie. She's new this year, and she's in your class. She couldn't make it to orientation day, so please show her around." He turned to the new girl. "Simone's been with us since Year Seven. You couldn't be in better hands." Mr. Collins glanced back to Hannah. "Be sure to give her the complete tour!"

Hannah's mouth dropped open as he spoke. She closed it again quickly.

"I'll see you both at assembly at nine o'clock," he concluded.

When Hannah didn't move, Mr. Collins added, "Go on, then. What are you waiting for?"

Hannah smiled at Julie, and with as much confidence as she could muster, led her toward the nearest building. She wished she'd paid more attention to the detailed maps Simone had drawn.

Oh well. She'd just have to figure it out as she went along.

———

"And this is the, uh..." Hannah pushed the door open a crack and peeped inside. There were large worktables in the center of this room, easels at the back, and paints and palettes on the shelves. "This is the art room." She flung the door open, allowing Julie to see inside. Then she led her along the corridor and up a flight of stairs.

To her right, a window revealed a room full of books. In case she'd had any doubts, the sign *Library* dispelled them.

"This is the library," Hannah declared, "and over there are the toilets." She pointed toward the restroom icons across the hall.

After passing one classroom after another and going back downstairs, they emerged once more into the open air and crossed the courtyard.

Here were the dance studios, each one fitted out with built-in barres and floor-to-ceiling mirrors on the front and back walls.

"Here are the studios," Hannah said.

Julie's face lit up as she peered through the windows. "They're fabulous, aren't they?"

The bell rang for the morning assembly. Sweeping Julie along in her wake, Hannah followed the other students.

They soon entered a building that turned out to be the theater, where assembly was held. The students sat in rows, laughing and chatting among themselves. Hannah could almost see herself dancing on the empty stage, could almost hear the applause. She could hardly wait for her first performance.

Then Mr. Collins marched onto the stage. He coughed softly into the microphone and the laughter and chatter died down into a respectful silence.

"Welcome back to the VSD," Mr. Collins began, "and a special welcome to our new students. Would you please stand up when I call your name."

Hannah cringed on behalf of the new students as they stood up, self-conscious and awkward, to polite applause.

When they were seated again, Mr. Collins continued. "I trust you are all refreshed, well-rested, and ready to work hard in the coming year. May I remind you that every year, hundreds of students audition for our school, and hundreds of students are turned away. You are the lucky few who have been selected. Don't take that opportunity for granted."

Hannah gulped as she listened, aware that she was the only dancer who hadn't auditioned, the only one there under false pretenses. She'd have to work twice as hard as everyone else to prove she belonged.

"All students are to check their dance schedules on the notice board," Mr. Collins was saying. "As you know, there will be no dance classes today. This morning you will have introductory academic classes, and then school is over for the day. Dance classes will begin tomorrow."

And suddenly, assembly was over, and Hannah found herself herded toward the exit. A minute later, she and Julie were out in the sunshine. Julie was soon lost inside a cluster of dancers, while Hannah's shoulders were squeezed, her back slapped, and her cheeks kissed by people she was supposed to know.

A short way away, a girl was waving. "Hey, Simone!"

Hannah waved back as she tried to figure out who this might be. Simone had said that she mostly hung out with her best friend Jess and a guy named Mitch. Jess, she knew, was half-Japanese, with straight black hair. Was this her, then? It could be, though in Simone's photos Jess had shoulder-length hair, and this girl's hair only reached just below her chin.

"Hi! Great to see you," said Hannah. "How were the holidays?"

"Not bad," said the girl, now close enough to give Hannah a hug. "Dragged a bit toward the end." She paused, then added: "So, what do you think of my haircut?" Definitely Jess, then.

"I love it," said Hannah, thinking that the photos she'd seen of Jess didn't do her justice. In real life, the petite and graceful girl had such delicate, exotic features.

Jess smiled. "How was Candance?"

"Great," said Hannah.

Jess looked doubtful. "That's an amazingly positive reaction for someone who didn't want to go."

Hannah winced inwardly. "I said that, didn't I?"

"Only every day for about three months. And in case you're suffering from some weird form of amnesia, you also said you didn't want to be a professional dancer."

"Hmm! Well, I've changed my mind."

"Why?" asked Jess, narrowing her lovely, almond-shaped eyes. "What happened at Candance?"

Hannah shrugged. "It's hard to explain."

"We'll talk about it later," said Jess. "Better not be late for class on the very first day."

# twenty-six

As Simone put on Hannah's Carmel College uniform—a navy-and-white-checked knee-length dress, white ankle socks, and black leather school shoes—she felt like she was playing dress-up. She hadn't worn a uniform since primary school, though in some ways she preferred it—no time wasted wondering what to wear. And if she didn't feel entirely comfortable at Hannah's school, at least she'd look like she belonged.

She was winding a navy ribbon through her hair when Manfred knocked on the bedroom door. "Good morning, Hannah."

"Morning, Dad," she called in return.

A moment later, Vanessa shouted up the stairs that breakfast was ready, her voice not quite drowned out by the music coming from Adam's room. Adam was singing along at the top of his voice and out of tune.

Simone smiled. She didn't mind the noise. It was friendly and warm.

After breakfast with the family—apple and sultana muffins

hot from the oven—she and Adam packed the generous lunches Vanessa had made and headed off, Kimmy whining when they left him behind.

Adam gave her one of his earbuds and together they listened to his choice of music as they walked to the bus stop on Dandenong Road. When the bus arrived, Simone followed Adam to the back, and after a twenty-minute ride through morning traffic, they reached Hannah's large and somewhat daunting school.

As she got off the bus, Simone looked around. To her right were vast ovals, and beyond the ovals, in the distance, were tennis courts. To her left, great expanses of dark gray asphalt stretched out to meet a sloping lawn, and beyond that was a children's playground. In front of her, spreading wide in both directions, were several buildings—single, double, and multistory.

Hannah hadn't prepared her for the size of Carmel College, and Simone had no idea which way to go. She'd asked Hannah to draw her a map, but Hannah had kept putting it off until at last she'd turned to her sister and said, "Quit worrying, Sim, it's not that hard to find your way 'round."

Now, for want of a better plan, Simone was about to follow Adam when someone rushed up to her, flinging sunburnt arms around her neck. "Hannah, it's so great to see you. I can't believe you didn't call."

This must be Dani, Simone figured—with mouse-brown hair as short and spiky as she'd expected, though Dani looked a little plumper than she had in the photos.

"Uh...sorry," said Simone, "but I only got back on Sunday night."

"Hmm! You still could have called. Come on, let's go see what class we're in." She linked her arm through Simone's and shepherded her toward one of the larger buildings.

Simone smiled to herself as she remembered something Hannah had said: "Dani likes to call the shots."

"You mean she's bossy?"

Hannah had laughed. "She prefers the word 'assertive.' But yeah, she has a tendency to take over, if you let her."

In this unfamiliar environment, Simone was happy for Dani to take the lead, and while Dani chattered nonstop, Simone struggled to make sense of all the references to people she hadn't heard of, let alone met.

It wasn't long before she found herself in a large hall with class lists and timetables pinned up on corkboards. She followed Dani until they reached the Year Ten ones.

"It figures," said Dani as she stared at the class lists. "I'm in 10F, you're in 10D. Why do they even bother asking us who we want to be with when they ignore what we say?"

"We can still hang out at lunchtime," Simone reassured her as she accompanied her up a flight of stairs and along a corridor.

"Hey, where are you going?" Dani asked her. "You're in Room 210. It's that way, remember?" She pointed vaguely in the opposite direction. "Meet me in the cafeteria at lunchtime?"

"Okay. See you then."

The morning passed quickly in a whirl of new faces and introductory classes. At the break, through a combination of trial, error, and plain good luck, Simone found her way to the office of Mr. Field, the level convener. The door was open, and he saw her even before she knocked.

"Come in," he said. "How can I help you?"

As Simone explained that she wanted to switch from Hebrew to French, Mr. Field gave her an unnerving appraisal.

"Why the sudden change of heart?"

"It's not sudden," said Simone. "I've been thinking about it for most of the summer."

Mr. Field scratched his head. "You're better off with Hebrew," he advised her. "The French class is already very full, but there are only..." He rifled through a stack of papers on his desk and consulted a list. "Only fourteen students in Hebrew. You'll get a lot more attention, and Mr. Aaronson is an excellent teacher."

Simone bit her lip and tried again. "I know he is, but... I'd rather do French. You see," she improvised, "I'm planning a trip to France when I finish school."

Mr. Field drummed his fingers on the desk while Simone held her breath. "What about your parents?" he said at last. "They signed off on Hebrew. Are they on board with this last-minute change?"

Simone hesitated only briefly. "Yes," she said.

"So you've discussed it, have you?"

Simone nodded.

Once again, the convener drummed a rhythm on the desktop.

"Madame Brun won't like it," he began.

"*Pleeease!*" said Simone.

Mr. Field sighed. "All right then." His tone was grudging. "I'll see if I can squeeze you in."

---

Day One was over at last, and Simone congratulated herself on having survived it. As she got off the bus at Hannah's stop, Adam pushed past her and tore down the street.

"Hey, Adam! Wait!"

He shouted something about soccer training and kept on running, and Simone ambled along the footpath, in no particular rush to get home.

"Have some fruit cake, Hannah," Vanessa called as she left to drop Adam off at soccer. "Dinner won't be for another two hours. Oh, and check your mail—I think there's something from Armadale Dance."

The letter from Armadale Dance, with timetable attached, informed her that classes would be starting the following week. She'd be dancing on Tuesdays and Thursdays after school, as well as four hours on Saturdays—just enough to maintain her technique and stay in shape.

She helped herself to some of Vanessa's homemade fruit cake, then went upstairs to do her homework. Shortly after she came downstairs again, Manfred arrived home, having collected Adam from soccer on the way.

"Hannah, how was your first day back at school?" He pulled Simone close, dropping a kiss on her forehead.

"Uh…great," she said. "How are things in publishing?"

"Excellent. We've got two terrific novels coming out next month. In fact," he said, opening his briefcase with boyish excitement, "I have advanced copies of both for my favorite daughter."

Simone smiled shyly as she took them. "I can't wait to read them." She surprised herself by reaching up to kiss his cheek. "Thanks, Dad."

Manfred beamed. "I can't tell you how delighted I am that you're finally developing an interest in books."

"She's growing up," said Vanessa, in a voice that sounded both puzzled and pleased.

Simone blushed, hoping that no one had noticed the flicker of guilt that crossed her features.

"Hannah," said Vanessa, interrupting her train of thought, "you've got a dentist appointment tomorrow at 5:00, so make sure you come straight home from school."

"But—"

"Don't look so worried. It's just a checkup."

# twenty-seven

Hannah pulled on Simone's flesh-colored tights and maroon leotard and threw a sundress on top. Then she rolled up the tights and slipped her feet into a pair of sneakers, as open-toed shoes were against school rules. She stood at Simone's mirror and fixed her hair. Now she looked the part of a full-time dance student.

It was Wednesday, her first full day at the VSD. The day before had been an odd one. She'd met her academic teachers and somehow survived a minefield of strangers. Today, though, she'd have to prove herself in the studio.

Harriet was squeezing oranges in the kitchen, and Hannah's hand trembled as she helped herself to a glass of juice.

"Simone, are you okay?"

Hannah nodded. "I'm always a bit nervous the first day of dance." She gulped down the juice and a serving of cereal, then stacked her bowl and glass in the dishwasher and said a hurried goodbye.

When she reached the VSD, Hannah's heart was hammering. Jess was already in the studio, pulling one leg back behind her and over her head. Beside her, Julie too was limbering up, pointing and flexing one foot at a time.

Hannah joined them and they exchanged greetings. Then, with one hand positioned lightly on the barre, she stood on her supporting leg and swung the other forward and back, forward and back. She counted to twenty, then turned to repeat the exercise with the other leg.

"How come we're only girls in this class?" Julie asked, looking around.

"We have separate classes for ballet," Jess explained. "Except on Fridays. But we're with the guys for all the other dance styles, as well as for repertoire and pas-de-deux. I'm so glad we've got Miss Sabto for ballet again," she continued.

"What's she like?" Julie asked, just as a tall redhead entered the studio. "Oh, is that her?"

"No," said Jess, "that's Miss Grunwald. She's the—"

"Pianist," Hannah guessed, as Miss Grunwald crossed the room toward the piano.

All the dancers fell silent as a small, thin woman appeared in the doorway, and with an air of authority that belied her size, strode to the front of the studio and addressed the class. "Good morning, girls. Before we begin, is there anyone new this year?"

Julie timidly raised her hand.

"Ah, yes, I remember your audition tape. You're the one from out of state. Have you met all your classmates?"

Julie nodded.

"Excellent! Then let's begin. I trust you've all been stretching over the holidays?"

There were nods and murmurs of assent all round.

"Good, then you shouldn't be too stiff. Still, as it's your first week back, we won't do anything too strenuous. Let me see two *demi pliés* with arms *à la seconde* and a *grand plié* bringing the arms to fifth." She nodded to Miss Grunwald, who began to play.

Rippling music filled the air and Hannah was swept along in its ebb and flow, allowing it to guide her to the heart of the movement.

As the dancers performed one barre exercise after another, Miss Sabto walked around the room, giving an occasional compliment or correcting her pupils.

"Nice work, Jess. Alison, those *tendus* are lazy. Push through the feet. Use the floor."

Hannah managed to escape comment until she began her *grand battements*. Then, under Miss Sabto's scrutiny, she felt herself trembling.

"A bit rusty, are you?" said the teacher.

Hannah nodded.

"Well, at least you're nice and supple," said Miss Sabto. "But don't cheat, Simone. Focus on alignment, not height. Let me see those *grand battements* again, and this time, don't throw your hip out."

---

"And now, an important announcement," Miss Sabto said at the end of the lesson. "The Bollywood dance we did last year was so well received that we've been asked to perform it at this year's Dance Spectacular. We only have a month to prepare, so we'll start to brush up on it next week."

Whooping and cheering, the dancers high-fived each other as they left the studio, thrilled at the chance to take part in the annual event that featured a range of dances performed by students from schools across Australia.

"Simone and Julie," called Miss Sabto, "I'd like to have a chat with you before you leave."

Hannah made her way toward the teacher, wondering what it was she'd already done wrong.

"Mr. Collins suggested you take Julie under your wing," Miss Sabto began, "and I think that's a really good idea."

Hannah exhaled slowly, relieved to know she wasn't in trouble.

Miss Sabto smiled at Julie, who was chewing a nail. "We have a buddy system," she explained, "and you won't find a better buddy than Simone. She's been here since Year Seven, and she knows the ropes." She turned to Hannah. "To start with, I'd like you to teach Julie the dance so she can perform it with the rest of you."

Already warm from class, Hannah felt herself break into a sweat. "The ... uh, dance?" she said, stalling for time.

"The Bollywood dance," Miss Sabto said.

For a second, Hannah toyed with the idea of saying she'd forgotten it, but then she nodded.

"I suggest you get started on it as soon as possible. The

quicker Julie learns it, the more polished she'll be. Here's a copy of the music," said Miss Sabto, handing Hannah a CD. "Studio 4 is always open for private practice."

After Miss Sabto had left the room, Julie gave Hannah a tentative smile. "I'm free at lunchtime," she said. "Or if you like, I could stay after school."

"This is a … really busy week for me," Hannah said. "Could we leave it till Monday?"

"I guess," said Julie, sagging a little.

"I'm really sorry," Hannah added.

"That's okay. I understand."

———

Hannah stared at the half-eaten peach in her hand, wondering just how she'd teach Julie a dance she'd never seen. She'd thought of asking Jess to go over it with her, but Jess would undoubtedly ask why she'd forgotten a dance she'd performed so many times.

At least she'd had the foresight to tell Julie she'd have to postpone it. Maybe Simone could run through it with her on the weekend. They'd have to find some way to meet up …

"Are you going to eat that," asked Jess, "or are you planning to just stare at it?"

Hannah sighed, resigning herself to the fact that she couldn't make any decisions until she'd talked to Simone.

"I hope," said Jess, her expression probing, "that you haven't changed your mind again about your dancing. You do want to be here?"

Hannah nodded. "More than ever."

Jess let out a dramatic sigh. "Well, that's a relief."

For a moment, Hannah forgot her dilemma as Matthew Holden crossed the courtyard. With his gray-blue eyes and sandy hair, he was easily the cutest guy in Year Ten if not all of the VSD. She perked up at the sight of him. She'd only spoken to him once or twice, but he seemed very friendly.

"You know," Jess was saying, "I never told you this, but you were so depressed at the end of last year I was really worried about you."

Matt was getting closer now. In a few seconds, he'd walk right by them.

"At one point," Jess continued, "I even thought about asking my mum to talk to yours about how unhappy you were. And some of the kids were taking bets on when you'd quit." She grabbed Matt's arm as he was passing. "Weren't they, Matt?"

"Sorry, what?"

"Last year," Jess repeated, "weren't some kids taking bets on when Simone would give up dancing?"

"Yeah," Matt said. He stopped and looked Hannah straight in the eye. "I'm glad you didn't."

"Really?" said Hannah. Buoyed by his interest, she flashed him a smile.

"Yeah, *really*. Not that I should have cared one way or the other," he added. "It's not like you ever gave me the time of day."

"Didn't I?"

"You know you didn't."

"Uh … sorry?"

Matt laughed. "You know, you're different this year … "

"Different how?"

"Well, don't take this the wrong way, but you used to be … a bit of a snob. You're friendlier now." He coughed with embarrassment. "Anyway, see you in hip-hop."

After he left, Hannah gazed after him, wondering why Simone had never mentioned this gorgeous guy. Had Simone really been unfriendly to him?

"You know, he's right," said Jess. "There *is* something different about you … "

Hannah changed the subject. "Do you think he likes me?"

"You'd have to be blind and deaf to ask. Matt's had a crush on you for years. Almost as long as Mitch has had a crush on him."

# twenty-eight

It was Simone's second day at Carmel College, and she and Dani were just entering the school building after lunch when she almost collided with a short, balding man with horn-rimmed glasses. He had begun to mutter an apology when recognition dawned on his face, and he growled at her in a foreign language. Simone stared at him blankly.

The man went red in the face and spoke again. This time Dani replied in the same guttural language, which sounded as if she was clearing her throat. She seemed embarrassed and gave Simone's arm a little tug.

Simone shrugged an apology, feeling sheepish. "Sorry," she said, her voice small.

The man grunted and went outside.

"Jeez, Hannah," Dani said, after he'd gone. "Why didn't you answer Mr. Aaronson? That was really rude."

Simone turned to Dani in despair. "I...my mind was miles away. I just...didn't hear a thing he said."

"He asked you why you dropped Hebrew and you completely ignored him."

"Did I? Oh, God!"

"What is it, Hannah? What's on your mind?"

Simone shook her head. "Nothing. I just…"

"You must have been thinking about *something*," said Dani.

Simone stared off into the distance. "There's this guy I met at Candance," she said at last, picturing Tom.

"Ah, now you're talking."

"He was pretty cute," said Simone, "and he…" She broke off suddenly. "I don't know why I'm telling you this. It's not like I'll ever see him again."

---

Mr. Field was right. Madame Brun was not happy to discover that another student had joined her class. She cast a grim eye over Simone as she took the roll.

"Why do you want to study French? *Pourquoi?* Your marks last year are not so good."

"My mother wanted me to drop French and study Hebrew," Simone said, in far better French than Hannah could have. "But I finally managed to convince her to let me do French. I think French is a beautiful language."

Groans and sniggers erupted around the classroom, but Simone sounded so well-spoken and sincere that Madame Brun beamed with approval. "*Oui, c'est vraiment une belle langue.* And what beautiful French you have, *ma cherie.*"

"*Merci*, Madame Brun. I practiced a lot over the holidays."

———————

Despite having made an ally of Madame Brun, it was hard to get through the rest of the day when the visit to the dentist loomed. Whenever Simone thought about it, a chill ran through her. If only she'd talked Vanessa into canceling...

But the dreaded appointment arrived, and now Simone reclined in the dental chair, mouth open, while Dr. Johnson prodded and probed.

"Fischer seal needs replacing," he said at last, "and put a watch on 5."

The dental nurse flipped through a pile of papers. "That's odd," she said.

"What is?" asked Dr. Johnson.

"According to Hannah's file, you filled that tooth in March last year, and the Fisher seal was replaced in September."

"Let me see that." Simone closed her mouth while Dr. Johnson studied the file. For a few long seconds all was quiet save for the low hum of the fluorescent lights and the tinny background noise of the radio.

"Someone's messed up," said Dr. Johnson. "This isn't her file."

"But there's her name," the nurse said, sounding flustered, "and we're always so meticulous with our records..."

"Not this time," said Dr. Johnson. "Files are subject to human error. Teeth, on the other hand, never lie."

"I don't see how this could have happened..."

Dr. Johnson lowered his voice. "Someone must have mixed up Hannah's file with somebody else's."

The smell of alcoholic disinfectant was suddenly nauseating, and Simone wished she could run away and disappear.

"If this gets out," the dentist told the nurse through gritted teeth, "the reputation of this clinic will be completely ruined."

"I realize that." The dental nurse sounded more frantic by the second. "But I honestly don't know—"

"It may have even been deliberate," Dr. Johnson was saying. "Someone's warped idea of a joke. Who's had access to these files?"

"I've no id … Wait," said the nurse, "it must have been that student nurse who was here last year."

"Well," said the dentist, "make damn sure she never comes back. And from now on," he instructed the nurse, "don't let anyone near those files." He moved back into Simone's line of vision to continue the checkup.

"Sorry about that," he said to Simone, his voice falsely cheerful. "I'll just give your teeth a clean before you leave."

Back in the waiting room, Vanessa was flipping through a magazine when Simone stepped out of the exam room, followed closely by Dr. Johnson. He called Vanessa over to them and spoke in a tone too low to be overheard. "I thought I should let you know myself that there was a slight mix-up with Hannah's file. But not to worry, it's all been sorted. She'll need another appointment in a month or so."

"Did he find new cavities?" Vanessa asked Simone after the dentist had gone.

"No. He just wants to replace my Fischer seal."

"Really? Didn't you have that done last…no, no, that must have been Adam."

———————

As soon as dinner was over, Simone escaped to her room. The "mix-up" at the dentist had left her feeling inwardly shaken. This time, she and Hannah had somehow managed to get away with it, but next time they might not be so lucky.

"I swear my heart was in my mouth," she said when Hannah called, "and I—"

"Don't worry about it," Hannah interrupted. "It worked out, didn't it?"

"I guess, but—"

"Listen, Sim." Hannah launched into a garbled story about having to teach some new girl a dance. "I don't see why she had to pick *me*, out of a whole class full of people who could have taught her."

"Okay, calm down," said Simone. "Which dance is it?"

"The Bollywood one. Do you know it?"

"Of course." It was a fast, tricky dance, full of classical leaps interspersed with traditional Bollywood moves: flexed feet, isolated head movements, thrusting hips, and intricate handwork. Simone had enjoyed it, although the teacher kept changing the choreography and it had taken weeks to learn it.

"Can you teach me?" Hannah asked.

"I guess, but—"

"Brilliant," said Hannah. "How about Sunday?"

"Where?"

"The botanical gardens?" Hannah suggested.

"What if it rains?"

"What choice do we have?"

They arranged to meet outside the kiosk in the botanical gardens, at two o'clock.

# twenty-nine

On Thursday, Hannah couldn't wait to get to school. After their morning break, the Year Tens would be starting pas-de-deux, in which they would learn to dance with a partner. Standing on the crowded tram, as the throng of city-goers jostled around her, Hannah imagined throwing herself into a risky fish dive, one leg bent beneath her, head just inches from the floor. Not that they would start with anything quite so dramatic. At least, not today... still, she smiled to herself in anticipation. Neither she nor the rest of her class had ever had proper pas-de-deux classes before—the lessons didn't begin until Year Ten, as only then were the boys considered strong enough to lift and support their female partners.

When the tram reached her stop, Hannah jumped off and flew down the street.

"Hey, Simone!"

She turned to see Matt sprinting toward her. She grinned and waved.

"What's your hurry?" he asked as he came up beside her.

"Pas-de-deux today," she reminded him. "I'm so excited."

"Me too," he said, as they entered the school. "I hope I get to dance with you."

————————

"Left hand on the barre, girls," Miss Sabto was saying, "and pull up tall. Imagine someone pulling a piece of string up through the center of your body and out of your head toward the ceiling."

Hannah felt herself becoming taller.

"Now," said Miss Sabto, "I'd like two *demi pliés* bringing the arm to first and back out to second, and a *grand plié* with the arm sweeping down and into first. Miss Grunwald?"

The pianist nodded and began to play.

"Lift the eye line, Simone. Don't look *at* the fingers, look beyond them. Alison, let me see those muscles wrapping."

The barre work continued, and Miss Sabto was meticulous and exacting, correcting every detail from the angle of the head to the position of the little finger. In return, she expected total commitment and dedication.

Hannah had never minded being corrected, just as she'd never minded demanding ballet teachers, for she knew that the stronger her technique, the better all-round dancer she'd be—but Miss Sabto was adjusting her position every minute. There was something unnerving about it, and it was a relief when the barre work ended and they moved to the center.

"When you perform a *port-de-bras*," Miss Sabto was

saying as the girls began their center work, "you should feel as though you're embracing the entire world."

Hannah put her heart and soul into capturing that feeling, and it felt as if there was indeed something inside her, something huge and unstoppable.

"That's it, Simone," said Miss Sabto. "That's really beautiful. You have a lovely flow."

It felt good to be singled out for doing well, but there wasn't time to savor the compliment because after that, the class became harder. The *petit allegro* was so fast she could barely keep up.

"Good work, everyone," said Miss Sabto, as the girls stood panting and catching their breath. "And now we're almost out of time. Would you rather finish with *grand jetés* or *fouettés*?"

"*Fouettés*," yelled one of the girls. "We haven't done them since last year."

"*Fouettés* it is, then," said Miss Sabto. "One at a time."

Jess performed sixteen beautiful *fouettés* in a row. Julie did four before losing her balance, and when Hannah's turn came, she managed eight.

*Not bad*, she told herself, glancing at the teacher to see her reaction. But Miss Sabto was watching her with a puzzled frown.

———————

"You're very quiet today," said Jess as she and Hannah entered the courtyard. "What's up, Simone?"

Remembering the expression on Miss Sabto's face, Hannah plunged in. "Tell me the truth—have you noticed anything different about my dancing?"

"Ah … different?" Jess hedged, but Hannah persisted.

"About my technique. Do you think I've regressed?"

Jess refused to meet her gaze. "It depends how you define 'regressed,'" she said. "To be honest, I'm usually too busy concentrating on my own technique to pay much attention to anyone else's."

"That's a cop-out. You saw my *fouettés*."

Jess squirmed. "You sure you want my honest opinion?"

"Absolutely."

"I think your technique isn't as strong as it used to be." Jess's words came out in a rush. "But I still think you're a fabulous dancer…"

"Go on," said Hannah.

"At first I thought it was a bit weird that your technique had slipped, since you danced over the summer, but then I figured it out."

"You did?"

"Uh-huh. You obviously had a teacher who told you to forget technique and focus on artistry and expression instead."

*Great theory*, thought Hannah. "I did," she said.

"And I think your teacher at Candance must have been really amazing," Jess continued, "if she helped you remember that dance is more than sore feet and aching muscles."

"She was," said Hannah.

Jess smiled. "Anyway," she said, "it's great you're into dance again. I'd miss you so much if you left the VSD."

———

Pas-de-deux was all that Hannah had hoped it would be. The class was taught by Mr. Dixon, who'd devised a series of exercises so successful that they were now well-known and used throughout the world.

"If you can master these," Mr. Dixon explained, as the captivated Year Tens watched the two Year Eleven students who had come in to demonstrate, "you'll be able to execute virtually any supported promenade, lift, jump, or turn that any choreographer throws your way. Now grab a partner."

Matt began heading in Hannah's direction.

"No, wait." Mr. Dixon held up a hand. "It's important to know how to establish a rapport quickly and easily with any partner, so we'll be changing partners fairly often. However, for this first lesson, it will be easier if I pair you up according to height."

Matt was paired with Julie, Hannah with Mitch.

"Lucky you," Jess said to Julie. "Matt's the best partner in the school. He's been doing ballroom dancing since he was five. Two years ago, he won the Victorian State Ballroom Championships for the under-fifteens, and now he's working toward winning in the open section."

"I thought it was against school rules to dance outside the VSD," Julie replied.

"It usually is," said Jess. "The staff here don't trust outside training. But in Matt's case, they've made an exception. They know he's got the best ballroom teachers in the country. He does ballroom every Saturday afternoon and three nights a week."

Hannah imagined being Matt's ballroom partner. A dreamy look came over her face as she pictured them winning competitions together. She wished she'd been partnered with him today.

Mitch tugged Hannah playfully by the arm, but she was still watching Matt, who gave her a disappointed shrug.

"Next time," she mouthed silently as she caught his eye.

Her gaze slid to Julie, whose height was exactly the same as her own. She couldn't help feeling a touch of envy, though she knew she had no reason to be jealous.

"Hey," said Mitch. "You've developed a thing for Matt."

"Is it that obvious?" Hannah asked.

"Only because I know you so well."

"It's agony watching him dancing with somebody else."

"Now you know how *I* feel all the time, and it's hopeless for me 'cause he'll never be gay." Mitch spun Hannah around in a lively twirl. "Don't know why *you're* complaining. He's liked you forever."

"Really?"

"As if you don't know!"

"Starting positions, everyone," called Mr. Dixon. "Now, let's see how well you've been paying attention."

---

After English, the last lesson that afternoon, Hannah headed for the tram. She'd loved every minute of her jam-packed day, but it had been a long one. Her stomach rumbled, and she wondered what Harriet was planning to make for dinner. She hoped it wouldn't be steamed fish and vegetables again. Though Harriet's meals were undeniably healthy, sometimes she felt like she'd been put on a diet. It made her want to lash out and overdose on ice cream and chocolate. Strange! She'd never felt like that before. The irony was that Harriet needn't be so strict about food. Hannah never gained weight; it didn't matter what she ate. The same would be true for Simone. Thinness was clearly in their genes.

A mechanical tune interrupted her thoughts. "Hello?" she said into Simone's mobile phone. There was no name on the caller ID.

"Simone, is that you?" The guy on the line sounded familiar, but she couldn't quite place him.

"Uh ... who is this?"

"Forgotten me already? I'm gutted," he said.

Now Hannah knew exactly who was calling. She collapsed onto a bench at the tram stop. "Hi, Tom," she said. "And no, I haven't forgotten. It's just ... I've never heard you on the phone before."

"That's true." She could imagine him smiling. "I'll forgive you this time. Anyway," he continued, "I'm calling to see if Saturday suits."

"Saturday?"

"We did say we'd get together back in Melbourne?"

"Uh ... right, we did," said Hannah quickly, "but I dance on Saturdays." She knew Simone would be spending a large chunk of her Saturdays at Armadale Dance, though she wasn't sure if it started this week or next.

"Sunday, then?" Tom suggested. "How about meeting at the entrance to Luna Park, two o'clock?"

"Sounds perfect," said Hannah, hoping the arrangement would suit Simone. "See you then."

Tom rang off just as Hannah remembered that two o'clock was exactly when she and Simone had planned to get together. She tried to call back, but a recorded message told her she was attempting to ring a protected number.

Darn! Now what would she do?

———

"Who's Tom?" said a voice. Matt slipped onto the bench beside her, and Hannah wondered how much he'd heard.

"No one," she said.

"He must be someone," he argued. "Didn't you just arrange a date?"

"Not really."

"You sure?" he asked, digging a playful elbow into her ribs.

"Why? Are you jealous?"

"Could be. Is he your boyfriend?"

Hannah shook her head quickly.

# thirty

Simone was just stepping out of the shower when she heard the ringtone she'd assigned to Hannah. Since they'd agreed only to call each other late at night, except in an emergency, her first reaction was to panic. She flung a towel around her dripping body and grabbed the phone. "Hannah! Are you okay?"

"Tom rang," Hannah began.

Simone felt herself becoming warmer. "He said he would."

"Yeah, I know, but I've done something stupid. I told him I'd meet him at two on Sunday—meaning *you* would— but that's when you're meant to be meeting me. Do you have any way of contacting him? Facebook? Email?"

"No," said Simone. "He was planning to deactivate his Facebook account before starting Year Twelve, and I don't have his email. How about the White Pages?"

"The number's not listed. I already checked."

"So," said Simone, "what do we do?"

"Well, you can't stand him up," Hannah replied. "Not now that I've arranged the date."

"No," said Simone, her pulse beginning to quicken. "I'll have to go."

"Ha! Don't pretend you're not dying to see him. But what about the Bollywood dance? When will you teach me? We're supposed to show it to Miss Sabto sometime next week."

"How about Saturday? Classes at Armadale Dance don't start till Tuesday."

"Yeah, but my VSD timetable has me dancing for most of the day. How about Sunday morning?"

"I can't," said Simone. "I've joined a study group with a bunch of kids from English Lit and I promised I'd go."

"But what about the dance, Simone? I'm really freaking out about it."

"Maybe you should just ask Jess to teach you."

"Then I'd have to tell her why," said Hannah, "and we agreed not to. But maybe we *should* tell our closest friends."

"No," said Simone. "You know what would happen. They'd each tell one other person who'd tell one other person —in the end the whole school would know."

"But—"

"Wait!" said Simone. "I know how you can learn the dance. Jess's dad filmed it at last year's concert. He put it on YouTube."

"Really?"

"I should have thought of that before. It's not ideal, but it's better than nothing. And you can watch it as often as you need to. I'll send you the link."

---

"Come over on Sunday?" Dani asked, on Friday at lunchtime. "I'm working on Saturdays now, sad to say."

"Can't," said Simone. "I've got English Lit study group in the morning, and—"

"*Study* group? Since when is studying more important than socializing?"

"And in the afternoon," Simone continued, ignoring the question, "I'm meeting up with that guy I told you about, the one from Candance."

Dani gave a resentful humph. "So you can't fit me into your busy schedule?"

Simone winced. "Sorry," she said. "Maybe some other time."

"Just *maybe*?" Dani pouted, clearly unused to not getting her way.

---

Simone's last lesson that day was Biblical Studies, which was compulsory at Hannah's school. It dealt exclusively with the Old Testament—the five Books of Moses and the commentaries that explained them. How strange it felt to discuss the Bible without referring to the New Testament and to Jesus. But the class was so interesting that it seemed like no time at all before the bell rang and the week was over.

"How was school?" asked Vanessa, when Simone and Adam came home.

"Great," said Simone. She hadn't expected to enjoy it so much, but Carmel College was very academic and she loved the challenge. The kids were thoughtful, intelligent, and interested in all kinds of things. It was a refreshing change from the VSD, where all anyone cared about was dance.

Simone helped herself to fruit, then set the table, remembering to use the good dishes and the fancy cutlery, since tonight was Shabbat, the Jewish Sabbath.

Not long after she'd showered and changed, Hannah's grandparents arrived, along with her uncle and cousins and a few family friends. Simone kissed their cheeks and said "Shabbat Shalom" like Hannah had taught her.

It was all a little overwhelming. Apart from Harriet's parents, who lived in Queensland and rarely visited, Simone and her mum only ever had guests for Christmas and Easter. But everyone was warm and friendly, and the atmosphere relaxed and happy.

Simone stood with the others while Manfred blessed the wine, and said "Amen" when everyone else did.

The food was delicious—though she'd never seen so much of it served at a single meal. Manfred carved the roast beef at the table, while booming a snatch of a well-known opera.

As Adam joked with his cousins, Hannah's parents laughed and chatted with their guests. How different they were from her own mother. Simone had barely thought of Harriet since returning to Melbourne, and felt a little guilty as she realized she hadn't missed her.

# thirty-one

Hannah arrived home on Friday to a disgruntled Harriet, who'd left work early with a headache.

"You forgot to wipe the kitchen sink this morning," she complained to Hannah. "And as for the state of your bedroom, I can't bear to look."

"Don't, then," said Hannah.

"Don't be so rude." Harriet folded her arms across her chest. "Just tidy your room."

"Why should I?" said Hannah. "Why do you care?"

"It's my job to care. I'm your mother, Simone."

"Well, maybe I wish you weren't," Hannah shot back, then clapped a hand over her mouth as she realized what a terrible thing she'd said. Harriet gasped, her expression changing from shock to pain.

"I didn't mean that," said Hannah. Her retraction was met with a hurt silence. She ran to her room.

Alone with her guilt, she thought about what she was missing at home. It was Shabbat tonight, and the house would be filled with family and friends. She felt so far away from them all.

———

She ventured out only when she needed to eat. Harriet was sitting at the kitchen table, scribbling numbers in a notebook.

"What are you doing?" Hannah hoped Harriet could hear the apology in her voice.

"Balancing the budget," Harriet said. "I still have some outstanding bills."

Hannah felt another pang of guilt. Maybe being a single parent wasn't easy. She shouldn't be adding to Harriet's problems. "How's your head?" she asked, wanting to make amends.

"It hurts," said Harriet, her tone frosty. She snapped the notebook shut. "I'm going to bed."

Alone once more, Hannah waited till it was late enough to call Simone, then haltingly told her what she'd done.

There was a brief silence. Then Simone said, "If you really want my mum to know you're sorry, ask her to take you to confession."

"*Confession!* Give me a break!"

"Do you want to get back in her good graces or don't you?" asked Simone.

"But—"

"Trust me, Hannah. It's not that scary. And Father Tim's a lovely man."

Hannah bit back another protest. "So, should I tell this Father Tim the truth?"

"Well, don't mention the fact that you haven't been baptized. Other than that, you can tell him anything. He's bound by the Seal of Confession. He won't tell a soul."

———————

On Sunday, sometime after morning mass, Harriet dropped her off outside the church. Hannah wished she didn't have to enter the imposing building. She'd never been inside a church before. But Harriet might mention something to Father Tim, and Hannah couldn't risk him saying he hadn't seen Simone. She braced herself and went inside.

There was something awe-inspiring about the church, with its high vaulted ceiling, cavernous spaces, and polished floor. The colorful stained-glass windows softened the light, and tall white candles added to the otherworldly glow. Flowers spilled out of enormous urns—roses, lilies, gladioli—and the scent of lavender mingled with the smell of incense.

From the moment Hannah stepped inside, guilt and curiosity welled up within her. She walked slowly down the aisle, her eye drawn toward a huge statue—a tortured Jesus on the cross. To the right was another, smaller statue—a serene Madonna, mother and child. A voice inside her said that this was idol worship, that she shouldn't be here.

"Sorry," she said to God. "Sorry for pretending to be Catholic." She wasn't sure whether she was addressing the Jewish god or the Catholic one.

The church seemed empty as she made her way toward

the confessional. Then a man who matched Simone's description of Father Tim approached her. Hannah tried to force a smile.

"Hello, Simone. Are you here for confession?"

Hannah nodded.

"No need to be nervous," the priest said gently. He drew the curtain aside and motioned her to enter the little booth.

She waited until she heard Father Tim enter from the other side, and the grille between them slid open.

"Yes, my child."

She took a deep breath and began the way Simone had instructed. "Bless me Father for I have sinned. It's been seven months since my last confession..." She broke off, not having rehearsed quite how she'd continue. She didn't have to mention Harriet—she could say what she liked.

"I...haven't been honest," she said at last. "I've been deceiving people. I...*am* deceiving people."

"Go on," the priest said gently.

"I...I've been pretending to be someone I'm not. And no one knows who I really am."

"Many people feel that way," Father Tim said softly. "God knows who you really are."

# thirty-two

It was hard to concentrate at the study group, and although Simone joined in the discussion of Shakespeare's tale of star-crossed lovers and mistaken identities, her mind kept wandering to Tom.

The morning couldn't end soon enough, and when it last it did, she rushed home, dumped her books in Hannah's room, and changed her outfit three times before settling on the jean shorts and crimson T-shirt she'd put on in the first place. She brushed her hair, leaving it lush and full.

She raced downstairs and grabbed two rice crackers and a bunch of grapes.

"Will you come bike riding with me?" Adam asked.

"Sorry, I can't. I already have plans." Then, seeing his disappointed look, she added, "Maybe next weekend." She regretted the words as soon as she'd spoken—she'd never owned a bike and hadn't learned to ride.

"Where are you going?"

"Running late," she mumbled, dashing past him. "Talk to you later."

———

Tom was standing outside the entrance to Luna Park and called out to her when he saw her arriving. "Hey, Simone!"

It was a relief to answer to her own name again. "Hi," she called, returning his wave. Since the first day at Candance, she'd felt a lurch of excitement every time she'd conjured his image—the shock of dark hair, the deep-set eyes, the attractive features and slightly brooding demeanor. She'd often wondered what it would be like when she saw him again, back in Melbourne. Now she knew—the giddy feeling hadn't diminished.

They grinned at each other and headed straight toward the beach, darting happy glances at each other as they ambled along.

"It's great to see you," he began.

"You too," she admitted shyly. "I didn't know what it would be like ... seeing each other back in Melbourne. I wasn't sure if ... "

"If what?" he prodded.

"If you'd still be interested ... "

"You did string me along," he admonished lightly. "But you were right," he said, a touch of laughter in his eyes. "It was worth waiting till we got back to Melbourne. It's much more fun when it's just the two of us."

They reached the pier and strolled barefoot along it, swinging their sandals by their sides.

"You know," he continued, "you really are different when you're on your own. That person at Candance, that girl who was so out-there in class and at lunchtimes, she didn't seem like the real you." He shook his head as Simone gave him an awkward smile. "Sorry," he said. "That must sound crazy. Talking as if you were two different people."

"No, I know what you mean. And it kind of makes sense because I'm a Gemini—sign of the twins. We're incredibly moody. What star sign are you?"

"Taurus. Down-to-earth and practical. I guess that's why I didn't argue with my parents when they suggested I dance less and focus on my studies. Although," he added, "I'm not sure I'd feel that way if I had your talent. Tell me again why you don't want to be a professional dancer."

Simone hesitated. One day she'd tell him about the awful stage fright, the constant exhaustion, the despair at having no way out. But not before he knew about her and Hannah. "A dancer's life is so … consuming," she said at last. "There are other things I'd rather do."

Tom gave her a quizzical look. "Then what's the point of going to the VSD?

Simone swallowed. "My mum still plans on me being a dancer."

"So … you haven't told her that's not what you want?"

Simone shook her head. "She's not the easiest person to talk to."

Tom frowned. "But shouldn't you be open with her?

Wouldn't she want to know what you think and how you feel? I know I do," he added. A sheepish expression crossed his face. "I can't believe I just said that."

"You want to know what I think and feel?" Simone's voice was small and shaky.

"I want to know everything about you," he admitted. "Every detail of your life before I met you, and every thought that's going through that interesting head."

"Interesting?"

"And beautiful."

They'd reached the end of the pier and stood on the edge, close but not touching, looking out at the endless horizon.

Simone felt his eyes on her as he turned his head to study her face, and her heart rate quickened.

"Tell me something about yourself," he said. "Anything I don't already know."

"I was adopted," said Simone.

"What's your favorite number?"

"Two." *Me and Hannah. Me and you.*

"Name one thing you value in life."

"Love," said Simone. "You?"

"Honesty."

Simone gulped and turned to look at him. Sunlight glinted in his hair, and her own face, seemingly ingenuous, was reflected in his trusting eyes.

———

Hand in hand, they walked back along the pier and sat down on the sand, their denim shorts and bare legs touching as they peered out at a tranquil sea.

From beneath her sunhat, Simone stole a glance at Tom's face, and her heart skipped a beat. She remembered lying by the pool in Canberra, certain she'd missed her chance to get to know him.

Tom turned toward her, and, like on the day she'd first seen him, caught her in the act of staring. A broad grin spread over his face. This time she didn't look away.

"Swim?" he asked. Without waiting for an answer he stood up, tossed his hat onto the sand, and stripped down to his trunks.

His lean body was smooth and toned, and for a second Simone was mesmerized, unable to speak.

"Race you," he said.

"Uh . . . okay." Simone pulled off her T-shirt and shorts to reveal a skimpy purple bikini.

"Wow!" he said.

Simone blushed. "Give me a head start," she said. "Your legs are longer."

Tom laughed. "Bet I still win. Ready?"

"Uh-huh." And Simone was off, running fast toward the sea.

He gained on her just as she reached the water's edge and he plunged in before her, turning back to drag her with him.

She held her breath as he pulled her under, and she came up laughing and gasping for air. The water reached her chest, lapping gently against her skin.

Tom surfaced beside her, his dark eyes shining.

*This day*, she thought, *could not get any better.*

A moment later they were facing each other, and he caught hold of her waist and leaned slowly toward her till his lips touched hers.

His kiss was perfect—soft and electric.

Simone had never been kissed before, and it was dream-like and magical and everything she'd ever imagined.

———————

Hours later, after the sun had dried them off, Tom gallantly offered to drive her home.

"You have a car?" Simone asked.

"A second-hand bomb, but it's better than nothing. You live in north Fitzroy, right?" Tom lived in Essendon, which was nowhere near Hannah's house.

"Um...yeah, but I'm not going home. I'm going to a...a relative's house in Armadale. I go there for dinner every Sunday night," she added, thinking ahead.

"Fine," he said. "I'll give you a lift."

There was something thrilling about sitting in the passenger seat of his old sedan. Even the streets looked different with him beside her—less mundane and more exciting. Simone wished the car ride would last longer.

When they crossed Dandenong Road, she asked him to park a street away. "If my relatives see you," she explained, "I'll be fielding questions all night long."

"No problem," he said.

"By the way," she added as he killed the engine, "my phone number's changed since we spoke on Friday."

Tom grinned and held out his arm. She thought of Candance and the first time she'd written her number on his muscled limb.

"I'll call you," he promised, as once again she scribbled a number on his skin. It still smelled salty from the sea.

After he kissed her goodbye—a long, lingering kiss that left her reeling—she watched the car till it disappeared.

———————

Simone sang in the shower as she thought of Tom. Now she knew what was meant by "whirlwind romance." She'd never expected things to move quite so fast. Too fast? Some people would say that kissing on the second date was much too soon—but somehow she felt like she'd known Tom forever. And of course, as far as he was concerned, he'd spent almost all day every day with her for an entire three weeks.

As she lathered her hair, she relived every moment of that wonderful afternoon.

She toweled herself dry and stared at her face in the bathroom mirror, wondering how she looked to Tom.

The phone rang, snapping her out of her reverie.

"Hello?"

"Missing you already," Tom was saying.

Simone's smile was so wide that her cheeks were aching. "Yeah, me too." She was glad he wasn't there to see her blushing.

They talked for nearly an hour and made plans to meet up again, same time same place, the following week.

Simone was still smiling when she put down the phone. She couldn't wait to call Hannah and fill her in on all that had happened. She made herself a cup of hot chocolate and brought it upstairs. Then, just as she was picking up the phone, a text came through from an unnamed sender:

I knw ur secret

A shiver of fear went through her, and Simone dropped the phone. It was several minutes before she calmed down enough to pick it up and call Hannah, but she was still trembling as she told Hannah about the creepy message she'd just received.

On the other end of the line, her sister was silent.

"It could be a mistake," Hannah said at last. "Maybe whoever sent that text intended it for someone else but got the wrong number."

"Maybe," Simone agreed, as unconvinced as Hannah sounded.

# thirty-three

Hannah had been growing increasingly frustrated. Learning a dance via YouTube was like studying a book with missing pages. Even though the Bollywood dance was synchronized, with the entire class performing the same movements at the same time, it was almost impossible to decipher the steps. Jess's dad was an amateur videographer, and his camerawork was uneven and erratic. When Hannah tried to focus on the footwork, the camera would suddenly zoom in on Jess's face. When she tried to work out just what the dancers were doing with their hands, the shot would swing to someone's feet.

On Sunday night, after they'd discussed that troubling text, Hannah had shown Simone, via Skype and webcam, the parts of the Bollywood dance she'd managed to learn, and Simone had tried to fill in the gaps. Still, the end result was nowhere near polished.

Hannah knew that Julie, too, had been disappointed, and though she was too decent to criticize, she was probably wondering why Miss Sabto had chosen Simone to teach her.

Now, not even forty-eight hours later, the Year Tens were rehearsing the dance, and Hannah along with Julie was a beat behind the rest of the class. Miss Sabto watched quietly, a concerned expression on her face.

"We'll go over this again tomorrow," Miss Sabto said, looking at Hannah. "The Dance Spectacular is just over three weeks away, and it has to be perfect. Our school's reputation is on the line."

She called Hannah over when the lesson ended. "Is everything all right at home?"

Hannah blushed and nodded.

"Because if there's anything you want to tell me, I—"

"I'm fine," Hannah interrupted quickly. "Everything's fine."

Miss Sabto sighed. "All right, Simone. But just remember, I'm here if you need me."

————————

During lunchtime, as Hannah and Jess passed the staff room, they overheard the teachers talking.

"How's the new girl coming along?" came the voice of the jazz teacher, Jenny Hill.

"You mean Julie?" That was Miss Sabto. "Oh, she's doing fine."

"They're a lovely bunch, those Year Ten kids, aren't they? And they're wonderful dancers."

"They are," said Miss Sabto, "though I have to say I'm

a little worried about Simone. We went over the Bollywood dance today. She gave such a patchy performance."

"Well, you have time for a few more rehearsals, don't you?"

"That's not the point. Don't you think it's a worry when the best dancer in the school suddenly has trouble remembering a dance she's done a hundred times?"

There was a strained silence in the staff room. Hannah froze outside the door.

"And it's not just that," Miss Sabto continued. "Simone could do thirty-two perfect *fouettés* by the end of last year. The other day, she only managed eight."

Hannah was devastated. She felt Jess place a sympathetic hand on her arm.

"Give her time," said the jazz teacher. "They always come back from the holidays a little rusty."

"She's more than a little rusty," said Miss Sabto. "She seems to have... forgotten things she knew."

"Maybe her mind's on some boy she met over the holidays and she's a bit distracted."

"I don't think that's it," came Miss Sabto's voice. "It's not that she isn't concentrating—she's actually trying very hard. She's just not the same dancer..."

"Well, maybe she's gone through a recent growth spurt. You know how that can throw them off."

"Could be," said Miss Sabto. "Not that I've noticed she's any taller..."

"Sometimes even small changes can make a difference—especially hormonal changes—and full-time dancers are often late developers."

"That's true. I was one myself. Even so," Miss Sabto added, "if she's not back on track fairly soon, we'll have to consider very carefully whether she should continue at this school, because once she enters Year Eleven—"

"Yes, yes, I know the rule," Jenny interrupted. "We can't ask them to leave because we can't disrupt their education at such a late stage. But if I know Simone, it won't be a problem."

"I hope you're right," said Miss Sabto.

———

Hannah flung herself onto the bench in the courtyard and buried her face in her hands. It was only when tears dampened her fingertips that she registered the fact that she was crying.

It wasn't fair. They expected so much of her, and all because... well, all because they thought she was Simone.

What would Miss Sabto make of her dancing if she knew the truth? A part of her wished she could tell her... but then she'd have to leave the school before the deception went any further, and she'd never get the chance to earn her place at the VSD.

Would she ever earn her place at this prestigious school?

Though she hadn't been there very long, Hannah was certain she wanted to stay. She loved everything about the VSD—from the grueling ballet training to the creative contemporary classes and the jazz and hip-hop, which were more like fun than work. She even liked the academic classes, which were smaller, friendlier, and less formal than those at Carmel College. Each morning she bounced into the studio at 8:05, and no matter how demanding her schedule, she still had a spring in her step at the end of the day. Brimming with enthusiasm, she'd firmly believed that confidence was all she needed. And she'd received so many compliments from the contemporary, jazz, and hip-hop teachers that it had seemed to be true.

Now, Hannah realized with a sinking heart that confidence alone wouldn't make her as good a dancer as Simone. She had to face the fact that she wasn't as accomplished as her talented sister and perhaps never would be.

Hannah blew her nose as Jess slid onto the bench beside her.

"Here you are," said Jess. "You ran off so quickly."

"Miss Sabto thinks I'm a terrible dancer."

"No, she just thinks your technique has regressed."

Hannah sniffed. "It isn't fair. Julie can only do five *fouettés* and she didn't do such a great job of the Bollywood dance either, but no one's saying she should leave."

"That's different," said Jess. "She's new here. She hasn't had your kind of training. Besides, don't you think you're overreacting? No one said you have to leave."

"I might have to, though," said Hannah, her lower lip beginning to tremble.

"Trust me, you won't." Jess put her arm round Hannah's shoulder. "You've got what every dancer wants—the perfect build. And you're a wonderful dancer. The teachers know that."

"Miss Sabto doesn't."

"She does. She called you 'the best dancer in the school.'" Was it Hannah's imagination, or was there a touch of envy in Jess's tone? "And anyway, she's just one teacher."

"Yeah," said Hannah, "the one teacher who really matters. Oh, Jess, I can't think of anything worse than being asked to leave."

———————

A little while later, Jess went to return some books to the library. Hannah sat slumped on the bench, alone, looking down when anyone wandered past. Then suddenly Matt was sitting beside her, touching her shoulder.

"Hey!" he said. "Jess told me about the conversation you overheard."

"Oh, great! So now the whole school knows what a rotten dancer I am." Tears welled up in Hannah's eyes and her vision blurred.

Matt put his arm around her and drew her to him. "Not true," he said. "I saw you were upset when you rushed out of the building, and I badgered Jess to tell me why. So you had a few off days," he continued. "Everyone knows you're brilliant."

Hannah sniveled into a tissue. "I'm not sure I am."

Matt took both her shoulders and turned her toward him. "Hey! You wouldn't be here if you didn't have talent. And you wouldn't have been given almost every class solo since you started Year Seven."

"Didn't you see how I stuffed up this morning?"

Matt began gently stroking her hair. "Maybe you've had a lot on your mind. Would it help if we went over the dance together?"

"You ... you'd do that for me?"

"Sure," said Matt. "I'll ask Miss Sabto for the music."

"I already have it," Hannah said.

"Great. Then let's meet after school in studio 4."

# thirty-four

With barely a glance in the mirror, Simone wound her hair into a bun with the speed and efficiency that came from years of practice. Apart from that first morning at Candance, it had been nearly two months since her last dance class. Though she hadn't missed the taxing routine, it might be fun to dance just a few times a week.

She checked the directions to Armadale Dance. It wouldn't take her long to get there.

"Do you want a lift?" Vanessa offered when Simone came downstairs, dressed in Hannah's navy leotard and flesh-colored tights, a shoestring dress thrown over the top.

"No, thanks. I'll walk."

The class began at half-past four, and Simone arrived with twenty minutes to spare—enough time for a decent warm-up. Swarms of girls charged through the crowded corridors of the school, greeting and hugging friends they hadn't seen all summer.

Simone recognized some of the faces from Hannah's

photos; others she'd never seen before. Doing her best to imitate her sister's warmth, she returned the hugs of total strangers and, attentive to their conversation, complimented one girl on her new hairstyle and told another how lovely her smile was now that she'd had her braces removed.

"Hannah, you got your ears pierced. Did it hurt?"

"A bit," said Simone, a small smile playing around her lips as she remembered Hannah's piercing shriek.

———————

It was strange to be back at the barre after such a long break, though in some ways it felt like she'd never left. Her years of training were so ingrained that when the teacher switched on the recorded music, her body knew just what to do.

A quick glance around the studio was all Simone needed to see that the girls had been grouped together according to age rather than talent or ability, and the difference in standard was huge. It was also clear that Hannah was a better dancer than any of them.

With her habitual focus and concentration, Simone worked her way through barre and center, only vaguely aware that while some girls were sneaking admiring glances in her direction, one or two looked like they wished they could tear out her hair.

She wasn't surprised. Every dance school had a few jealous, competitive girls, and she was used to ignoring them. And though she hadn't intended stealing the limelight, she couldn't avoid it—she was too good a dancer.

Her technique was clearly stronger than Hannah's, and though she didn't want to arouse suspicion, she simply wasn't capable of dancing badly.

Luckily, Hannah had told her dance teachers that she'd be attending Candance, so a marked improvement wasn't wholly unexpected.

"You've made huge progress at that summer school," Miss de Sylva said, watching Simone perform a series of pirouettes. "You must have worked hard."

# thirty-five

Hannah sat through French, the last period of the day, without taking in a word of the lesson. She was thinking about all that had happened since the morning, when she'd performed the Bollywood dance so poorly that she'd made Miss Sabto wonder whether she should even remain at the school.

The teacher's words had come as a shock, and Hannah had begun to doubt her ability. Yet somehow, Matt had restored her self-belief with his offer to help with the dance. It had to be perfect by the time Miss Sabto saw it again. No way would Hannah leave the school before having a chance to prove she belonged. She'd just have to work harder.

But as she copied French verbs from the Smart Board, she squirmed. Even though Matt had been nothing but kind and supportive, he'd seen her at her most vulnerable; it would be so humiliating to face him again.

God, he was gorgeous! That luscious sandy hair! Those incredible blue-gray eyes! She blushed as she recalled the way he'd run his fingers through her hair, and her body hummed at the memory.

The bell rang and the lesson ended. Hannah tossed her French books into her bag and made her way to Studio 4.

———————

Picking up choreography had always been one of Hannah's strengths, and now that she had Matt to teach her, she had no trouble mastering the intricate dance. She was feeling more confident by the minute, and knew she would perform it well at the next rehearsal.

After running through the dance three times in a row, the two of them collapsed on the studio floor, breathless and panting.

"Thanks for doing this," Hannah said when she was able to speak.

Matt grinned. "Don't think my motives are entirely selfless. I'd hate to see you leave the VSD. Especially now you've dropped your ice-maiden act."

Ice maiden? How could Simone be so misunderstood?

"At least you know it was an act," said Hannah, suddenly wanting to defend her twin. She remembered what Simone had said about her constant exhaustion, her performance anxiety, the terrible stage fright, and how she'd come to loathe the VSD. Of *course* Simone had seemed antisocial. And given that she'd had the best roles in almost every performance, it was easy to see why her classmates might have thought her a bit standoffish.

Hannah murmured under her breath, "She was just shy."

"She?" asked Matt.

"I ... I think of who I was then," Hannah said quickly, "almost as if I were a different person. I used to be shy. But in the summer, somehow I came out of my shell."

"I'm glad you did," said Matt, standing up and pulling Hannah to her feet. "Hey, let's go over the stuff we learned in pas-de-deux. Got your pointe shoes?"

"Uh-huh."

They took up a position in the center of the studio, and Matt stood behind her as she rose onto pointe, lifted one leg into a *développé,* then pivoted into an *arabesque.* He supported her through an *arabesque penchée* as she lifted her leg higher still, her head tilting down toward the floor, then sliding back up. Releasing one hand and placing it securely beneath her thigh, he lifted her, and before Hannah knew it, he was carrying her across the studio floor.

Light, ethereal, beautiful—she couldn't have said exactly how she felt. She could see why Matt was such a popular partner. His touch was gentle but firm, and though she brimmed with a sense of excitement and daring, she still felt safe and natural in his arms.

He brought her back down and into a double *pirouette,* his hands resting gently on her waist as she completed the turn. Then she jumped, dartlike, into the air, and he spun her so that she turned to face him, looking down from above as he looked up at her.

With Hannah's torso secure in his hands, he drew her slowly down toward him until she was standing on one pointed foot, the other curled behind her ankle. Their heads were almost level now . . .

Time stood still as they held their positions.

And somehow he bridged the distance between them, and kissed her.

She kissed him back. And she would have fallen if it weren't for his strong arms holding her up.

———————

The school was deserted by the time they left. They walked to the tram stop hand in hand, jostling and bumping each other along the way. Hannah's tram came first, and when she climbed on board, Matt watched her until the tram receded and she was no longer in his line of vision.

In North Fitzroy, she got off the tram in a happy daze. Streets that had once seemed cold and drab looked warm and inviting. It was hard to believe that just a few hours earlier she'd felt so low. Now her veins were fizzing with adrenaline and a renewed determination to claim her place at the VSD.

She surprised herself by hugging Harriet. Going to confession had helped to ease the tension between them, as Simone had predicted. Since then, Hannah had been making an effort to be tidy, and Harriet was a little less critical and more relaxed.

"Good day?" asked Harriet.

"The best," said Hannah, picking up the phone to call Julie, who answered on the second ring.

"Julie? I'm sorry I did such a lousy job of teaching you the

Bollywood dance. But I've gone over it again, and I remember it now."

They arranged to meet the following morning an hour before warm-up. Then Hannah went back to dreaming of Matt.

# thirty-six

"You said you'd go bike riding with me," Adam accused.

"No, I said *maybe*." Simone felt a stab of guilt when she saw his disappointment, but she was meeting up with Tom today and she had to get going. "Sorry, Adam. I already have plans."

"You *always* have plans."

Simone let out a frustrated sigh. Dani had called that morning to invite her over for the second time, and she'd ranted a bit when Simone turned her down. Now it was Adam giving her grief.

"Sorry," she repeated, a hint of annoyance in her voice. It wasn't *her* fault Adam was at loose ends. "We'll hang out together some other time."

Vanessa's car pulled into the drive as Simone was leaving.

"Hannah, where are you off to?"

"I'm meeting a friend."

"Which friend?" asked Vanessa lightly.

"Someone I met at Candance," said Simone.

"Lovely," said Vanessa. "Have a nice time."

———————

Tom waved to her as soon as he saw her. "Simone! Over here!"

Once again, it was a relief to be able to answer to the name "Simone." Being Hannah had its rewards, but it was also stressful. At least with Tom, Simone felt able to be herself. And after disappointing both Dani and Adam, it was good to finally be with someone she didn't feel she was letting down.

Her heart rate quickened as she hurried toward him. Though she could count the hours they'd spent together, in some ways it felt like she'd known Tom forever. He was both enigmatic and familiar—would she always feel a little light-headed at the sight of that rakish mop of near-black hair, that intelligent face, and those deep, dark eyes?

He greeted her with a quick kiss, then slung his arm around her shoulder. Simone slid hers around his waist and they turned as one toward the beach, inhaling the salty sea air carried by a gentle breeze.

They walked happily and quietly along the shore, the shallow water erasing their footprints even before they were fully formed.

Tom was the first to break the silence. "I like seeing you like this," he said.

"Like what?" Simone asked.

"Relaxed and happy. Hey, I hope I haven't jinxed your mood. As soon as I said that, you tensed right up. What is it, Simone?"

"Nothing," she said, with a quick shake of her head. "It's just..."

"What?"

Simone swallowed. "I don't want to pretend with you," she said carefully.

Tom smiled. "Good to know."

"I know I seem different at different times, but—"

"Everyone does," Tom interrupted, "depending on their mood and who they're with. Different hats for different occasions."

"Yeah, but I want you to know that..."

"What?" he asked.

Simone stopped walking, allowing the hand that had circled his waist to drop to her side. "That the person you see right now is the real me. Just remember that. Please."

He picked up her hand and gave it a squeeze. "You know what? You think too much."

They walked on in silence till they reached a café on the beach, overlooking the water. "Want a drink or an ice cream?" he asked.

Soon they were sitting on plastic chairs in the shade of a beach umbrella, sharing a milkshake. Simone sipped slowly, fighting the temptation to tell Tom everything. She'd never had a boyfriend before, and she wished there were no secrets between them.

*I have a sister,* she could say. If only it were that easy! But the truth wasn't solely hers to reveal. She and Hannah were in this together. Besides, no matter how lightheaded he made her feel, it just didn't seem right that Tom or anyone else should know the truth about her and Hannah before they told their parents, who'd loved them and raised them.

So she said nothing, focusing instead on enjoying the icy sweetness of the strawberry milkshake as it tickled her throat.

Tom was watching her intently.

"What?" she asked.

"I just like looking at you," he said with a grin. "You have hidden depths. God, that sounds like such a cliché, but in your case it's true."

*Hidden is right*, Simone thought, cheeks flushing. "Everyone has hidden depths, including you," she said.

"You think so?"

"I do."

He rose to the challenge. "Okay, then. I'll tell you anything you want to know. Ask me a question."

"Ever had a girlfriend?"

"Once," said Tom, "for nearly a year. We broke up six months ago."

"Why?" asked Simone.

Tom looked out at the sea for a long moment before turning back to her. "She lied to me," he said at last. "Turns out she was also seeing some other guy. I knew I'd never be able to trust her again."

Simone thought she saw a hint of pain.

"But I'm glad we're not together any more." Tom's voice softened as he added, "Because now I have you." He took her chin in his hand. "More questions?" he asked.

Despite the compliment she'd just received, Simone

thought it was time to lighten the mood. "What's the most embarrassing thing you've ever done?"

Tom slurped the last dregs of his milkshake and gave her a grin. "Pick an easy one, why don't you?"

---

"Don't you think it's an amazing coincidence that we've both got boyfriends at the same time?" Hannah was saying on the phone. "I just love the synchronicity of it, don't you?"

"Actually, I read it's common with identical twins." Simone snuggled deeper under the quilt, preparing for a lengthy chat. "After all, our DNA's identical; maybe we're genetically and biologically programmed to develop an interest in guys at a certain age."

"Don't know," said Hannah. "I mean, it's not like we want the same things in other areas of our lives. We're not one person."

"No, we're not," said Simone, "but in a way we *are* one entity. We're like two sides of the same coin—the same, but different…"

After she said good night to Hannah, Simone closed her eyes and, as on the previous Sunday night, relived every minute of the afternoon she'd spent with Tom. She'd almost reached their parting kiss when the phone beeped and a message came through. She reached for it eagerly. Maybe he was texting a final good night.

I knw wat ur up to.

So much for Hannah's theory that the first text had been a mistake!

Once again, there was no Sender ID.

———————

"So who do you think it could be?" Simone asked when she'd finally stopped pacing and called Hannah back.

"You tell me. Is anyone acting suspicious around you?"

"Not that I've noticed," said Simone. "Maybe it's someone at the VSD."

"It couldn't be, Sim. No one there would have my number."

Though the bedroom door was firmly closed, Simone lowered her voice as she climbed back into bed. "It might be a teacher. Mr. Aaronson seemed pretty annoyed when I dropped his class. Maybe he's figured the whole thing out..."

"No way," said Hannah. "Teachers don't have access to students' private mobile numbers. And even if they did, no teacher would behave in such a juvenile way."

Hannah was right. A teacher would come straight out and confront the culprit. Besides, it was unlikely a teacher would suspect the truth when Hannah and Simone's own parents didn't.

"It must be some jerk in our year," Hannah continued.

"But we've been so careful," said Simone, her voice full of anguish.

"Maybe it's someone's idea of a joke."

"Not very funny though, is it? What about Dani?" Simone asked. "Would she be capable of something so spiteful?"

"She *can* be a bit possessive," Hannah replied, "and she might be annoyed if she thinks you've dumped her for the sake of some guy. But Dani's not scared of confrontation—if she was angry, you'd know."

"Right," said Simone. "Anyway, how *could* she know about the swap?"

"I don't know, Sim, but *someone* must..."

Simone's stomach clenched with renewed fear.

Hannah finally said good night, but Simone lay awake, too fretful to sleep.

# thirty-seven

Despite occasional flashes of anxiety over the two text messages Simone had received, Hannah floated through the following days hardly aware there was solid ground beneath her feet. She'd had crushes before, but never like this. This kind of thing only happened to other people. She hadn't expected it to happen to her—at least, not now, not yet.

Was it her imagination, or was Matt becoming even better-looking with each passing day?

During breaks and lunchtime, Hannah and Matt had become inseparable. Never one to abandon her friends, Hannah made sure that she and Matt often ate lunch with Jess and Mitch, after which those two would find an excuse to leave.

"I hope I haven't been ignoring you," she said to them one day.

"You haven't," said Jess.

"Maybe a bit," Mitch countered, "but I understand. Someone had to snag Matt, and if it couldn't be me, it might as well be you." He punched her lightly on the arm. "I really mean that."

"The only thing is..." Jess began. "Remember what we heard Miss Sabto saying in the staff room that day?"

As if she could forget a single word of that conversation!

"She was worried some boy was distracting you."

"Actually, that was Miss Hill," Hannah corrected.

"Whatever," said Jess. "Anyway, she might have a point, so you'd better make sure that doesn't happen."

"It won't," said Hannah. Far from being distracted by Matt, she knew she was working better than ever. All her teachers had praised her, and yesterday she'd managed twenty-four near-perfect *fouettés*. She and Matt rehearsed together almost daily after school, and when they finished rehearsing, he taught her popular ballroom styles—Samba and Foxtrot, Tango and Jive.

Hannah had gained so much confidence that she'd almost stopped worrying about whether she was a good enough dancer for the VSD. She knew she belonged. She'd even become accustomed to answering to the name "Simone." And after all, what did it really matter what her name was?

"Well, you'd better be careful," Jess warned her again. "Don't take your talent for granted."

"I wouldn't. I don't."

"You used to," said Jess. "When you were the best in the year, you never appreciated it. It was only when you started to struggle that you decided you wanted to stay at the school."

What was her point? Was Jess, as Simone had maintained, simply a concerned and caring friend? Or was there a trace of resentment in her tone? Had she been jealous of Simone's flawless technique? Was it easier for Jess to be her friend when Simone was unhappy or no longer appeared to be top dog?

The VSD was a competitive school, where even close friends were rivals. And though Hannah had never imagined that anyone at the VSD could have heard of Hannah Segal from Carmel College—let alone know her phone number or that Simone and Hannah had swapped lives—she wondered now if she'd been wrong. Might Jess have sent those scary texts? Could she know that Hannah wasn't Simone?

"But hey," Jess was saying. "I'm glad you're here, and I think you and Matt make an awesome couple." Jess's face was open and honest—and Hannah felt more certain than ever that whoever had sent those disturbing texts wasn't a student at the VSD.

With Matt's help, Hannah's problems at the VSD had been all but solved, and she was determined to enjoy her dream school for as long as she could. She refused to be side-tracked by some spiteful person with a mobile phone.

---

Now that she'd perfected the steps, Hannah couldn't wait for the Dance Spectacular the following week. The final dress rehearsal, which was held at the magnificent State Theatre in Melbourne's Arts Centre, had gone so well.

Hannah and Matt left the Arts Centre in high spirits and strolled down to Southbank, through the Sunday market and along the river. They passed the food court and shopping complex, the restaurants with their balconies and patios overlooking the sparkling water, and the outdoor buskers—singers, magicians, fire-eaters, and pantomime artists dressed as silver or gold statues, barely moving.

Suddenly famished from the morning's rehearsal, they walked back to the crowded food court and made their way over to the baked potato bar and stood in the queue.

A familiar voice caught Hannah's attention.

" ... can't decide between the Mexican and the Mediterranean topping," the voice was saying.

Instinctively, Hannah spun around. She found herself face to face with Dani, the best friend she hadn't seen in months. A huge grin spread over her face, and she stopped herself from saying "It's so great to see you" just in time.

Dani was with a couple of other girls from Carmel College. She grinned back at Hannah and her eyes grew wide as she looked pointedly from Hannah to Matt and back to Hannah. That look said it all:

*Who is he? Is this the guy from Candance you were telling me about?*

*Where have you been hiding him?*

*Why haven't I met him yet?*

*When were you planning to introduce me?*

"Hi," said Dani and her two companions.

"Uh ... hi," said Hannah. "This is ... " Had Simone ever mentioned Tom's name to Dani? Just in case, Hannah thought better of introducing Matt by name. "This is ... my boyfriend."

"Hi," said Matt, putting his arm around Hannah's waist as if confirming his status.

*Please*, Hannah prayed inwardly, *don't mention school or homework or anything else that might give me away*. She threw her friend an I-really-want-to-be-alone-with-my-boyfriend look, hoping Dani would get the message.

Dani did. "You know," she said to the girls who were with her, "I don't think I want a baked potato. Let's get crepes instead." She leaned in and whispered in Hannah's ear, "I'll expect a *thorough* debrief at school tomorrow."

"You're on," said Hannah. "Bye, you guys."

"See you later, Hannah," Dani called as she and the two other girls disappeared into the crowd.

"That was weird," said Matt.

"What was?"

"She called you 'Hannah.'"

"Um...yeah, she always does. She thinks I look like Hannah Montana."

———

Matt carried their tray of spuds piled high with toppings to a vacant table. Sliding into the seat beside him, Hannah thought about telling the truth: *Actually, she called me Hannah because that's my name.*

Matt lifted a forkful of potato and coleslaw and gave her a smile. "You've got this strange look on your face. What's on your mind?"

It would be so easy to tell him. Matt would be sure to

keep it a secret if she did—at least, he'd try. But even with the best intentions, what if he accidentally called her "Hannah" in front of their friends—or worse, a teacher? No, it would be best to say nothing. That way he couldn't inadvertently slip up and give her away. Besides, it wouldn't be fair of her to confess to Matt when Simone had managed not to confide in Tom.

Hannah shrugged. "I'm too hungry to think." She slipped a forkful of beans and potato into her mouth, and for the next few minutes they ate with zest while Hannah pretended that nothing was wrong.

Privately, though, she'd started to worry. What if Matt somehow discovered the truth before she told him herself? He'd no longer trust her, and he'd think she hadn't trusted him.

# thirty-eight

Wandering through the botanical gardens hand in hand, Simone and Tom climbed the path that meandered up the hill. When they reached the top, they paused for breath, taking in the magnificent view—the city in the distance and the lake below.

"Hungry?" asked Tom, and Simone nodded. They veered off the path and onto the lawn, choosing a spot where the grass was rich and deep. Simone sighed happily as she kicked off her thongs and sank onto the thick, green carpet beneath her feet.

"Impressive," she said, as Tom uncovered the picnic lunch. He'd made the sandwiches himself—tuna and lettuce wedged between crusty rye. He'd also brought juice and a thermos of tea.

When they'd devoured every morsel between them, they lay back on the grass, looking up at the sky. Wispy white clouds floated through the sea of blue. "It's another world up there," Simone whispered softly. "That one looks a bit like a castle."

"And that one," said Tom, pointing to a puff of white edged with silvery gray, "looks a lot like a dancer. Which reminds me..."

"What?"

"I've been meaning to ask you...why didn't you tell me the VSD is performing at the Dance Spectacular?"

With that one question, Simone's peace of mind was quickly destroyed. She fought down panic and nausea and tried not to sound worried as she answered. "I didn't think it was important. How did you know?"

Tom looked across at her and grinned. "I looked up the VSD website. I've been waiting for a chance to see you perform."

Simone sat up and tugged at a handful of grass, uprooting the blades. "I'd rather you didn't."

Tom sat up too, crossing his legs and propping his chin in his hands. "Why not?" he asked.

"Because I..." She looked at him awkwardly, tension thickening the air between them.

"Are you ashamed of me?" he asked.

"Of course not."

"Because sometimes it felt like that at Candance. I...I thought we'd moved on."

"We have," Simone whispered, watching a clod of earth come out in her hand.

Tom frowned. "Like I've said before, I love being alone

with you. But I hate the idea of being a secret. I want the whole world to know we're together."

"I get that," she said. "I'd just rather you didn't come to the Dance Spectacular. I…" *I'm not going to be there.* "I'd be too nervous with you there."

"Would you? Why?"

"I'm not… myself when I perform. I don't like who I am when I'm on the stage." It felt so good to say that out loud.

Tom looked confused. "At Candance you seemed to love performing."

"That was just summer school," Simone replied. "It didn't feel like a real performance. But the Dance Spectacular's a really big deal."

He picked up a strand of her hair and twirled it gently. "If you'd really rather not be up there on that stage, all the more reason for me to support you. Isn't that what boyfriends do? Support their girlfriends?"

A troubled expression crossed Simone's face. "Only if their girlfriends want them to," she said at last.

There was an awkward silence.

Tom packed up the remains of the picnic and hoisted the basket onto his shoulder. "Come on, let's walk some more." He held out his hands to help her up and she took them, glad to feel his skin on hers.

"You know," he said, as they continued walking, "one of these days you're going to have to have that conversation with your mum."

"I know," said Simone, "but I hate confrontation."

"You should tell her sooner rather than later."

Simone shook her head. "It's not that simple...look how hard *you've* been working just because your parents want you to get into law."

"That's different," said Tom. "If I really believed law wasn't for me, I'm sure they'd respect that. What you do with your life should be up to you."

"Not sure that's true. Remember how I told you I was adopted?"

Tom nodded.

"Well," said Simone, "my mum could have left me in the orphanage. She didn't. She chose to adopt me, and she...she's sacrificed so much for me that I...I hate the idea of disappointing her."

Tom lifted her hand and kissed her thumb. "Number one," he said, "you won't get through life without disappointing people. People will all want different things from you, and there's no way you'll be able to please them all. And number two," he added, unfurling her index finger to kiss that too, "she *chose* to adopt you. She was probably dying to have a child."

"That's what *she* says."

"There you go. But you're missing the point. If she chose her path in life, why shouldn't you get to choose yours?"

Simone sighed. "Maybe I'm not meant to choose."

"Why not?

"Because I haven't been given a choice about anything. I didn't *choose* for my birth parents to die before I was born. I didn't *choose* to be adopted." *And I never chose to be separated from my identical twin.* "If I never had a choice, maybe I'm just not meant to have one."

Tom shook his head, incredulous. "That's crazy. No kid has a choice. No kid decides whether his parents will live or die. To some extent we're all victims of fate. But we still have choices…"

They'd reached the butterfly enclosure, which promised an enchanting world of flight and color. "You may be right in theory," Simone said as they went through one gate after another, "but it doesn't change the fact that I don't *feel* I have the right to choose."

"Then I'll have to work on you until you do," said Tom. "I'm glad you trusted me enough to tell me, though."

––––––––––––

Hours later, Simone lay in bed with the phone pressed to her ear, smiling up at the ceiling as she once again listened to Tom saying how much he missed her during the week.

"At least we've got Sundays," she told him.

"But not next Sunday," he said. "You'll be at the Dance Spectacular." He paused, then asked, "Are you absolutely positive you don't want me there?"

"Uh-huh. No offense." They burst out laughing. "You know, I can hardly remember what I used to do on Sunday afternoons."

Tom chuckled. "Me too. I guess next Sunday I'll hit the books, which, come to think of it, I should be doing now. I've got a test tomorrow."

"Good luck," she said.

"Thanks," Tom answered. "I'll call you tomorrow."

"'Night," said Simone.

"Sweet dreams," said Tom.

---

Hannah called as soon as Simone had said good night to Tom. "You'll never guess who I bumped into."

Simone laughed. That was so typical of Hannah—jumping straight in, not even bothering with a *hello* or *how are you*. "Who?" she asked.

"Dani. She saw me with Matt. I had to introduce them."

"Uh-oh. She knows my boyfriend's name is Tom."

"Don't worry," said Hannah. "I didn't mention Matt by name. I introduced him as 'my boyfriend.'"

Simone let out a sigh of relief. "Still, he looks nothing like Tom."

"So? Dani hasn't seen Tom, has she?"

"No, but I've described him to her, and there's no way Matt would fit that description."

Hannah laughed. "I wouldn't worry too much about that. Everyone knows that love is blind. Anyway, I just thought I'd better warn you. Oh, and by the way, Dani wasn't alone." As Hannah named the girls Dani had been with, Simone's mind was racing ahead to the explanations she'd have to give for the discrepancies between the guy she'd described and the one they'd all seen.

"I left Dani with a promise I'd fill her in on all the details tomorrow in school," Hannah was saying. "So you'd better figure out what you're going to say. She won't let you off the hook—you know what she's like."

"I think I'm beginning to," said Simone.

"Anyway, Sim, I had the most amazing day."

Simone smiled. "Me too. Except for one tricky moment when Tom mentioned the Dance Spectacular next week and said he wanted to come. I convinced him not to."

"Phew," said Hannah.

"But I can't stand not telling him the truth."

"I know how you feel. I wish I could be up front with Matt. If anything, it's harder for me because I see him daily. I hate not being honest with him. Sometimes I come so close to blurting the truth."

"Well, make sure you don't," Simone said quickly. "Once something gets out at the VSD ... But it's different with Tom. Who could he tell?"

"You never know," said Hannah. "You just never know."

The two girls were silent for a while.

"As long as I'm not telling Tom the truth," Simone said at last, "I feel like he doesn't really know me."

"Why?" asked Hannah. "Do you think someone has to know everything about you to know who you are?"

"I guess," said Simone.

"But that's just not true. For fifteen and a half years you didn't know you had a twin. Does that mean you didn't know who you were?"

"It might," said Simone.

"It doesn't. You are who you are."

Simone let out an audible sigh. "I just wonder if he'd still like me if he knew about you."

"Of course he would," Hannah replied. "It's not like you become a whole other person when you're with him. And as long as I'm not around to confuse him, he *is* getting to know the real you."

Simone twisted a strand of hair around her finger. "Tom has a real thing about honesty. And he's right. For a relationship to work, there has to be trust. I think that's what's bothering me. As long as I withhold the truth, I feel like I'm betraying his trust."

"You're not betraying his trust. You're just not giving him yours. But you will, eventually. We both will—eventually."

"Yeah, well maybe 'eventually' isn't soon enough. In the meantime, whoever sent those spooky texts could ruin everything."

"Do you think I don't know that?" said Hannah. "Honestly, Sim, we're—"

The telephone beeped and Simone cut her off. "I've got a call waiting. It's Dani—I'd better go. Time for damage control."

"Hannah!" said Dani when Simone took the call. "No wonder you've been hiding your boyfriend all this time. He's really cute. Although," she continued, "he's not exactly the guy I imagined. Didn't you say his hair was black?"

"It was," said Simone without missing a beat. "He dyed it for the summer holidays. Now he's gone back to his natural color."

"He's totally into you," Dani said. "How come he never texts you at school?"

"He calls me at night," Simone answered truthfully. "During the day he's too busy with his studies. Did I mention he's doing Year Twelve?"

"Really? He doesn't look any older than we do."

Simone could have kicked herself. "Yeah, well, looks are deceptive."

Vanessa knocked on the door, then peered inside. "Hannah, don't you think it's time you got some sleep?"

"I heard that," said Dani. "Your mum wants you to get off the phone."

"She does," said Simone. "It's been a really busy day."

"'Night," said Dani. "See you tomorrow."

# thirty-nine

Backstage at the State Theatre, the air buzzed with excited tension as the Year Ten dancers in their bright Bollywood costumes dashed around hugging their classmates, wishing one another luck.

"A little decorum please, Year Tens," said Miss Sabto. "And save your energy for the stage."

"It's amazing how you're totally over your stage fright," Jess said to Hannah. "I guess you've got Matt to thank for that."

Hannah smiled in agreement. "Yeah, I guess I have."

"Go get 'em, Simone," said Mitch, stopping to give Hannah a hug before rushing by.

"Is there time to pee?" asked Julie, nervously jumping up and down.

"If you're quick," said Jess. "Good luck," she added.

"Julie, where do you think you're going?" a frowning Miss Sabto called to Julie's retreating back.

"The bathroom," called Julie.

"Well, hurry *up*. You should have gone before. Where are the rest of the boys?" Ah, here they are now."

Matt crept up behind Hannah and covered her eyes. "Break a leg, Simone."

"Matthew Holden!" said Miss Sabto, shocked. "*Never* say that to a dancer."

Matt and Hannah burst out laughing before giving each other a quick hug that turned into a fierce embrace. Then they took their places.

"Silence, everyone, or they'll hear you from the audience," hissed Mr. Dixon.

Julie rushed back just as the Bollywood music began. Jess gave Hannah a thumbs-up.

Hannah returned the gesture, then took a deep breath, her face flushed beneath her makeup, adrenaline rushing through her veins. It was hard to believe she was about to perform at the most prestigious venue in the whole of Melbourne.

The Bollywood dancers burst onto the stage to a roar of applause. Looking striking in her genie-style costume—arms, feet, and midriff bare—Hannah threw herself into the dance with unparalleled passion and pure concentration, her elation infectious.

Magic happened; her body flew through the dance with a knowledge that transcended her mind's awareness. When the dance ended and she left the stage, she couldn't remember performing the steps, but her exhilaration remained.

"Fabulous job, Simone," said Miss Sabto, smiling warmly.

---

Hannah left the dressing room and headed for the St. Kilda Road entrance to the theater. The Dance Spectacular had been a huge success, and families who'd watched their kids perform mingled happily on the Arts Center steps and in the courtyard below, waiting for the dancers to come out of the building and talking about how wonderful the production had been.

Not all the VSD parents had turned up, since the Year Tens had performed the Bollywood dance at the VSD's annual show the previous year. Harriet, stage mum that she was, had wanted to come, but Hannah had convinced her that it wasn't worth paying thirty-five dollars to watch a dance she'd already seen.

It was Sunday, and the show had ended at three o'clock. Hannah floated down the steps of the Arts Center still on a high. She'd nailed the dance, Miss Sabto had admired her performance, and she had the most adorable boyfriend on the planet. If only her parents had seen her up there on that stage!

She caught her breath, all thoughts of parents entirely forgotten as Matt appeared at the top of the stairs. He ran lightly down and sprinted toward her. They came together like two magnets, kissing slowly as the world disappeared.

For a few seconds, life was perfect.

"Damn!" said Matt. "I've left my phone in the dressing room. I'd better get it."

"I'll come with you," Hannah said.

"No, I'll have to make a run for it before they lock the door."

Hannah watched as he dashed inside, then turned back toward the street.

Maybe her eyes were deceiving her. She closed them tightly for a moment, then opened them slowly and looked again. No, her eyes had not been deceiving her. Tom Delaney was walking toward her. What the bejeezus was he doing here?

Simone had said that Tom knew about the Dance Spectacular and wanted to come, but that she'd convinced him not to. So he hadn't come to the actual performance, yet here he was, arriving now, probably hoping to surprise her...

Well, he'd surprised Hannah all right, and he was looking at her with an expression of hurt mixed with anger. She knew at once that he's seen her with Matt.

Tom reached her before she had a chance to gather her thoughts.

"So *he's* the reason you didn't want me to show up today." Tom's voice wavered as he spoke. "And I thought it was because you were modest, or shy."

Hannah blanched. "It's not what you think."

"I saw you *kissing* him, Simone."

Hannah could have kicked herself. If only she'd been more discreet! "I can explain," she said, wishing she could replay those last few minutes, take back that kiss.

And then Matt was back, holding his phone up like a trophy, but his grin faded as he noticed Tom.

There was an awkward silence. Then Hannah said, "Matt, this is Tom."

The two boys appraised each other with ill-concealed hostility.

Then suddenly Mitch appeared on the scene, grinning at Tom. "Tom Delaney!"

Tom mustered up a smile for Mitch.

"You know him?" asked Hannah.

Tom nodded, refusing to glance her way. "Mitch and I used to go to the same dance school." He clenched and unclenched his hands, and his voice was strained. "So how's it going, Mitch?"

While Tom struggled to make small talk with Mitch, Matt pulled Hannah aside. "Simone, what's going on?"

"Nothing," said Hannah.

"That's him, isn't it? The guy on the phone, that time I asked if you were setting up a date?"

Hannah nodded.

"He's obviously into you. This is war."

Hannah sighed. "Matt, there's no competition."

"Then why is he here? And why is there so much tension between you?"

Hannah opened her mouth, then closed it again.

"Just tell me, Simone."

There was so much to say, and it was all so long and complicated. How should she begin? And where? What if he was furious she hadn't told him sooner—so furious that he refused to keep the truth a secret?

Matt was watching her with a semblance of patience, but a palpable anger simmered beneath it. It was too great a risk, Hannah decided, to own up now—surely she should wait until he'd calmed down and was in a better mood. In any case, she couldn't confide in him without consulting Simone.

She stood twisting her fingers, avoiding his gaze.

Matt waited several long seconds for an explanation. When none was forthcoming, he spun on his heel and walked away.

"Matt, wait!"

But he was already striding toward the street.

———————

"You've been two-timing both of us," Tom said, after Matt and Mitch had gone.

Tears pricked Hannah's eyes and she blinked them away. "I haven't," she said.

"Why can't you just admit it? I *saw* you, Simone."

*I've made a mistake,* Hannah thought. *I should have told them both the truth.* But it was too late for that. She'd already messed things up with Matt, but maybe it wasn't too late to salvage Simone's relationship with Tom. She'd just have to hope he could keep a secret, and that he wouldn't be mad ...

She took a deep breath. "There's something I have to tell you," she began.

"Save it," said Tom. "I thought we could trust each other, but I was wrong. You're not the person I thought you were."

Before she could say another word, he'd walked off in a huff.

For a few seconds Hannah just stood there, tears coursing down her cheeks. All around her, people still in high spirits from the show were talking and laughing. She alone was an oasis of silence amid the noise and clamor. How quickly this wonderful day had turned to disaster!

# forty

Though Simone had known she wouldn't be seeing Tom that afternoon—after all, he thought she was performing at the Dance Spectacular—she'd expected to hear from him some time that day. But when hour after hour passed with no phone call, no voicemail message, and no texts either, she began to suspect that something was wrong.

Then Hannah had called and filled her in on everything that had happened, prefacing her words with "Promise you won't be mad." And how could she be, when it was clear that Hannah had been put on the spot—she couldn't have known that Tom would turn up right after the show. Things were a mess, but Simone didn't think she would have handled matters any better than Hannah did.

Still, several days later, the fact remained that Tom hadn't called. She missed the sound of his voice and their long, rambling conversations. She missed the way he listened to her as if what she said really mattered. She missed his arms around her, the warmth of his skin...

She threw herself into books and schoolwork, spending twice as long on her essays and assignments as she had before. And when Manfred brought home advance copies of books yet to be released to the general public, she finished them quickly and asked for more.

At first, Manfred and Vanessa seemed delighted that their daughter was taking her schoolwork so seriously. Then one evening, when Simone was sitting at her desk, buried in Shakespeare, Vanessa knocked softly on the door.

"Hannah, is something wrong?"

Though Simone appreciated the Segals' warmth and concern, having to answer to the name of Hannah was becoming a strain. She wished she could integrate her new way of life with the person she truly was, and stop pretending.

If only she hadn't pretended with Tom! Apart from Hannah, he was the only person who'd called her "Simone" on a daily basis. And now he might never say her name again.

Once again, she wondered whether she should call him to tell him the truth, and once again, she dismissed the idea. It was hard to believe he'd forgive her when she knew how much he valued honesty. He probably thought honesty didn't matter to her, or that she didn't think him capable of keeping a confidence.

Hannah had said that she'd tried to talk to Tom at the time, but that he wouldn't listen—he'd walked away. That rankled. If Tom really cared about her, he'd have given Hannah a chance to explain. And though a part of her felt that *he* was the victim, somehow she couldn't help feeling betrayed.

"Hannah?" Vanessa was still standing in the doorway, quietly watching Simone.

"Sorry, what?"

"Is something wrong?" Vanessa repeated.

Simone slowly shook her head, but she knew she wasn't fooling Hannah's perceptive mother.

Vanessa remained in the doorway a moment longer, then said good night and walked away.

Simone tried to focus on the play she'd been reading, but thoughts of Tom ruined her concentration.

"Hey, sis?" This time it was Adam in the doorway, wearing pajamas, hair wet from the shower.

"What?" asked Simone.

"Midnight feast in my room? Nine o'clock?"

Sweet of him, but Simone preferred to mope on her own. "Sorry. Still studying," she said.

Soon after Adam had left the room, Simone changed her mind. Hanging out with Hannah's younger brother might be just the therapy she needed. She snapped the book shut.

Adam had forgotten to close her door, and the sweet, nutty aroma of the almond crescents he and Vanessa had been baking wafted upstairs. Simone's phone beeped just as she was heading out of the room, and she ran back in to check the message.

I knw wat ur hiding. Own up or i'll tell.

Adam and the nine p.m. midnight feast instantly forgotten, Simone texted Hannah with trembling fingers.

Urgnt. Jst got text msg #3. Call me ASAP.

This latest message, the third so far, was downright intimidating.

Her heart in her mouth, Simone paced the room. She waited anxiously for Hannah to call, the thought of being busted made worse by the realization that, after all their efforts to keep their identities secret, they'd have lost their boyfriends for nothing if the truth was revealed now.

Neither Simone nor Hannah had given much thought to how long their deception would continue, or how they would end it. It was scary to think that now the decision might not be theirs to make.

––––––––––

Later that evening, Simone slipped quietly down to the kitchen. She was pouring herself a glass of juice when she became aware of a murmur of voices. Manfred and Vanessa were in the study, talking quietly, and she would have ignored them had she not caught the name "Hannah" spoken in muted tones. She strained to hear the conversation.

"But she spends so much time alone in her room. Isn't that unhealthy?" Vanessa was asking.

Manfred's voice was reassuring. "I'd say that's pretty normal for a teenage girl. Though never having been one myself, I can't be sure."

"I just wish she'd confide in me," Vanessa replied.

"Teenagers don't confide in their parents," Manfred said. "They confide in their friends."

"Do you think she might have confided in Adam?"

"I doubt it," said Manfred.

"But they were always so close." A brief silence ensued, then Vanessa continued. "I have a feeling there's a boy involved. When I was a teenager, I spent hours pining over boys who didn't know I existed."

"In that case, they must have been either very blind or very stupid. Lucky for me that they were."

Vanessa chuckled.

Simone smiled wryly and crept upstairs.

Her thoughts turned to her mother as she climbed into bed. If she was worried about how Tom would react when he learned the truth, what about Harriet? That was something she didn't want to think about—but Harriet would find out, eventually.

She'd gotten herself into this whole mess in the first place because she'd lacked the courage to confront her mother. Now the confrontation would be so much worse, because it wasn't just a matter of letting Harriet know she couldn't become a professional dancer—she'd have to deal with the consequences of having deceived her all this time.

Simone had wanted a break from the VSD—but she'd also wanted, she realized now, a break from her mother.

Did that make her a horrible, ungrateful daughter?

Would Harriet ever understand?

# forty-one

If someone had plunged a knife in her chest, Hannah didn't think it could hurt any more. Maybe the physical pain would be a relief. Matt had avoided her all week, and when he was told to partner her in pas-de-deux, he held her with obvious reluctance, visibly recoiling from her touch. When she spun to face him, he steadfastly refused to meet her eye. The pair were so clumsy together that Mr. Dixon finally told him to dance with Julie instead. "You'd better get over whatever disagreement you've had with Simone," the teacher added, clearly annoyed. "Dancers don't have the luxury of allowing personal issues to interfere with their work."

Both in and out of class, Matt did his best to stay away from Hannah, just as Tom was refusing to contact Simone. But while Hannah could understand Tom's behavior—he thought it was Simone he'd seen with Matt—Matt's animosity didn't make sense. Hannah wasn't sure what she'd say to Matt if given the chance, but she never had the opportunity;

whenever she tried to approach him, he veered off in another direction.

To make matters worse, it wasn't just Matt who was treating Hannah like a leper. Mitch was also giving her a wide berth, disappearing whenever he saw her coming but not before throwing a contemptuous glance her way. Even Jess seemed torn by divided loyalties, her attitude toward her friend lacking its usual warmth.

"What have I done?" Hannah said to Jess. "Why won't Matt even talk to me? And why's Mitch treating me like I've got the plague?"

Jess groaned in frustration. "Like you don't know."

"I don't," said Hannah.

"Tom told Mitch," said Jess. "On Sunday, after the Dance Spectacular. And Mitch told Matt."

"Told him *what?*"

Jess sighed dramatically, as if Hannah were deliberately trying her patience. "Tom told Mitch that he met you at Candance and that he's been seeing you every Sunday ever since. He said you were *his* girlfriend—at least he thought you were. What did you expect, Simone? How did you think Matt would react when he found out? Or did you assume he wouldn't?"

"But it's not true," Hannah protested. "I haven't been meeting up with Tom. I haven't seen him once since Candance."

A flicker of doubt crossed Jess's features.

"Jess, don't you believe me?"

"I want to," said Jess.

"Please," said Hannah. "I'm not the sort of person who would two-time a guy."

"No, you're not," Jess admitted. "At least, you weren't. But you're so different this year, I sometimes feel I don't know you at all."

———

For a few interminable days, Hannah spent breaks and lunchtimes wandering the campus alone. Was it her imagination, or had the story of her "treachery" spread throughout the school? She couldn't be sure, but it seemed she'd become the subject of a dozen whispered conversations. The small campus, which had seemed so warm and inviting, had suddenly turned friendless and claustrophobic. For the first time since starting at the VSD, Hannah longed for Dani and her other friends at Carmel College. If only life could go back to how it was the week before!

If she tried telling Jess, Matt, and Mitch the truth, they might not listen or believe her. And even if she could trust them with so huge a secret, she wasn't sure how they'd react to having been lied to all this time. Confessing now might make things worse.

In class, she was unable to concentrate. When Miss Sabto instructed her to grow tall and light, she couldn't do it. She felt as if a heavy rock had lodged inside her.

And it wasn't just her classical dancing that was suffering, either.

"Simone," said Mr. Dixon during rehearsal for a contemporary piece, "this is a joyous dance, not a funeral wake. Don't look so glum."

Whenever Hannah thought of Matt, which was most of the time, her dancing suffered even more. If only he weren't ignoring her. If only he'd give her a chance to explain. Still, if the quality of her dancing depended on somebody else, then she clearly wasn't as good a dancer as she'd hoped.

For the first time since arriving at the VSD, she was so unhappy that she seriously considered telling Simone she wanted to swap back. At least then she could face her defeat in the cocoon of home.

But how could she drop Simone back into the mess that she, Hannah, had created? No, Simone had suffered enough already at the VSD. It wouldn't be fair.

Besides, if they swapped back now, what would she have accomplished? What would the past few months have been for? Hannah hadn't quite given up on her dream of becoming a dancer, and though she doubted her talent and ability, she still entertained a vague hope that somehow it would all work out…

But as teachers cast worried glances in her direction, she had to admit that her grand adventure was becoming a nightmare.

"Simone," said Harriet one evening, "are you okay?"

Hannah nodded briefly, mumbling something about having had a bad day. Harriet was probably the last person she'd dare to confide in.

At night she hid her misery from Simone when they talked on the phone, though Simone was the one person who would understand. And Simone too was miserable—Tom still hadn't called.

When the phone call ended and Hannah found herself alone in her sister's bed, exhausted but unable to sleep, she yearned for home. She wanted to snuggle up in the crook of her mother's arm and be on the receiving end of one of her father's bear hugs. She wanted to wrestle Adam for the remote control, or sing along with the younger brother who'd always looked up to her no matter what.

Bunching her pillow to her damp cheeks as she tossed and turned in the darkened room, Hannah thought of Kimmy and his way of sensing when something was wrong. She longed to feel him nuzzling up against her, watching her with large, dark, knowing eyes.

She thought of the comfortable home she'd always had, and the wonderful family...

She'd been so focused on her goals that she hadn't considered how her actions might affect others, how they might react when they learned the truth about what she'd been up to these last few months.

A shudder went through her as she tried to imagine how they might feel.

Would they understand, empathize, and forgive her behavior? Or would they be angry?

What if they never loved her again?

# forty-two

When Manfred and Vanessa arrived at Carmel College with Simone, the three headed straight to the multipurpose hall where Simone had collected her timetable on her very first day. Although nearly a month remained till the end of term, the hall was now set up for parent-teacher interviews, which were well underway. About thirty-five desks stood at regular intervals behind a notice board that displayed the names of the teachers and where they were sitting. In front of the board, students and their parents mingled.

Simone clutched her schedule of appointments while Manfred and Vanessa studied the seating plan. A bell rang, and there was a flurry of movement as teachers abruptly concluded their five-minute interviews and parents moved on to their next appointment.

Simone marveled at the well-organized system. At the VSD, parent-teacher interviews were haphazard affairs, with lots of jostling in crowded classrooms and pushy parents slipping in ahead of others who'd been waiting longer. Here, the interviews ran like clockwork.

"Show me that list again," said Vanessa.

"Our first appointment's with Mr. Field," Simone replied, passing her a printed sheet filled in by hand.

"Your level convener?"

"Yes," said Simone. "He's supposed to give an overview of each student's performance and ask the parents if they have any general concerns."

"And have we?" asked Manfred, his eyes twinkling.

"I don't think so," said Simone.

Vanessa wrinkled her forehead as she studied the schedule. "You seem to have forgotten Mr. Aaronson."

"Um, no. I didn't forget him. I don't have him this year."

"Really? But I'm sure I signed off on Hebrew," said Vanessa, frowning.

"You did," said Simone, "but I switched to French. I thought I told you."

Vanessa threw Manfred a questioning look.

"It's the first I've heard of it," said Manfred, "but I thought she should do French all along. It's not as if she's planning to live in Israel. And think about all the French references in literature," he began, launching into one of his favorite topics. "When you understand the linguistic connections between French and English, you get so much more out of—"

"Hannah," said Vanessa, cutting him off, "you were the one who picked Hebrew."

"I know I did," Simone replied. "But I changed my mind. I agree with Dad—I think French will serve me better."

"*Serve you better?* You know, your spoken expression really has become more sophisticated," Manfred said, beaming approval. "It must be all that reading you've been doing lately."

"But didn't I buy you the Hebrew textbook?" Vanessa was asking.

"I swapped it for the French one at the school bookshop," Simone explained. "It wasn't a problem."

The bell rang again and a burst of human traffic added to the general swell of noise.

"Come on," said Simone. "It's our turn now."

As they crossed the floor to the desk where Mr. Field was sitting, Simone noticed how different the teachers seemed with parents around. They were all so determinedly cheerful that it was almost impossible to imagine them growling at students.

"Mr. and Mrs. Segal, and Hannah," said the level convener, shaking first Manfred and then Vanessa by the hand. "Please take a seat." He flipped through a list of teachers' comments. "Well," he began, "I think you'll be very pleased with Hannah's progress. It appears she's become a serious and conscientious student, and less of a chatterbox than she used to be. Her teachers tell me she's quiet, thoughtful, and cooperative. She's working extremely well in all her subjects, and has even topped the class in French..."

"So, how did your parent-teacher interviews go?" Adam asked when Simone returned.

"Fine," said Simone.

"You're lucky they're over and done with," he said. "Mine aren't till the last week of term, and I bet my teachers will say horrible things."

Simone leaned over and ruffled his hair. "Nah," she said. "How bad could you be?"

"Don't do that," he said, pulling away. "Don't treat me like I'm four years old."

"Sorry," said Simone, surprised at how offended he seemed.

"Hannah?" said Vanessa. "Don't forget that tomorrow you've got another appointment with Dr. Johnson for the Fischer seal."

# forty-three

Embarrassed by how badly she was dancing, Hannah instructed herself to focus. But when her turn came to perform a series of *fouettés*, she lost her balance almost as soon as she began. She started over, and stumbled again.

Miss Sabto said nothing. She didn't need to. Never before had Hannah had such a strong desire to be invisible. Aware of the mixture of smug and pitying looks directed her way, she wished she'd stayed in bed that morning instead of coming to school.

"Don't forget to write your names down for the parent-teacher interviews," Miss Sabto told the class at the end of the lesson. "As your dance convener, I'll be reporting on your progress in all your dance subjects."

During the morning break, Hannah tried not to think about the upcoming parent-teacher interviews and the poor report she was bound to receive. She bit into an apple, but found she could neither taste nor swallow.

Julie saw her throw it in the bin. "Hey, Simone! Are you okay?"

"Actually, no. I'm having a really lousy day."

"Come outside, then," Julie suggested. "Hang out with me."

Hannah managed a grateful smile. "Thanks," she said, "but I'd be rotten company. Maybe later." She couldn't trust herself with Julie. Another kind word and she'd burst into tears.

After Julie had gone, Hannah wandered past the staff room and caught the tail end of a conversation.

"So that's it, then," Miss Sabto was saying. "We'll have to ask her to leave the school."

It was official, then. Hannah's fears had been realized. The worst had happened. She had failed. She willed herself to move, but couldn't.

Suddenly the staff room door opened and Miss Sabto stepped out. She took one look at Hannah's face, put an arm around her shoulder, and steered her into an empty classroom. She sat her down gently at one of the desks.

"Tell me what's going on, Simone."

Perhaps the time had come to reveal the truth. If she said nothing, then at the parent-teacher interview Miss Sabto would suggest to Harriet that her daughter leave the VSD. And while Simone might be happy to do just that, she should be able to do it openly and honestly, with her head held high. Simone should not have to skulk away in shame because of Hannah's failure.

But if she confessed, she'd have to deal with the consequences—it would be too late to change her mind.

Hannah buried her face in her hands. Whatever she said or did, nothing would change the dreaded outcome.

Should she tell Miss Sabto who she really was?

One way or another, their parents would soon learn the truth.

If Hannah didn't tell Miss Sabto now, while she had the chance, whoever was sending those ominous texts might tell her first—or tell Manfred and Vanessa, or Harriet.

But if she did own up, perhaps Miss Sabto would be able to help. She had to trust *some*one.

"Simone?" The teacher's voice was full of concern.

Hannah plunged in.

"I'm not Simone," she murmured softly.

"Sorry?" said Miss Sabto.

"I said, I'm not Simone. I'm her sister, Hannah."

---

Hannah showed Miss Sabto a photo of her and Simone, taken at Candance and stored on her phone. When she finished explaining how she and Simone had met and discovered they were identical twins, the teacher still looked a little dazed.

Hannah went over the story again, this time more slowly, adding bits of information she'd overlooked in her first, rushed attempt to get it all out.

"Weren't your parents … suspicious?" Miss Sabto finally asked.

"Not really," said Hannah. "Simone and I swapped as much information as we could about each other's lives. And we're pretty sure our parents didn't know they'd adopted an identical twin."

"Still, don't you think swapping lives was rather a … drastic thing to do?"

"I do," said Hannah, her face twisting in anguish. "But Simone was desperate to leave the VSD, and I'd always wanted to come here. I thought if I was confident enough, and worked hard enough, I could prove I belonged." Tears welled up in Hannah's eyes. "But now everything's gone wrong and … " The tears slid unhindered down her cheeks.

Miss Sabto placed a comforting hand on Hannah's shoulder and produced a box of tissues. Hannah took a few, then blew her nose and wiped her face before continuing. "I miss my family so much, and I don't know if they'll ever forgive me. And now you're going to ask me to leave, and I—"

"Hang on a minute," said Miss Sabto. "Who said anything about leaving?"

Hannah choked back a sob. "I heard you. I was passing the staff room, and—"

"You jumped to conclusions." Miss Sabto's voice was an odd mixture of accusation and reassurance. "That conversation had nothing to do with you. I was talking about another student."

"You were? But this whole week, I—"

"Performed poorly, I know. I'm aware of the recent friction between you and … certain members of the class. But dancers are only human, and you're still a student, a teenager.

I can't expect the same degree of professionalism from you as I would from an adult dancer, despite what Mr. Dixon might say. Hannah," said Miss Sabto, "you clearly have talent."

Hannah felt a glimmer of hope. "You really think so?"

"I do," said the teacher.

"But... I'll never be as good a dancer as Simone."

"I wouldn't say that," Miss Sabto countered. "You have the same physical facility as Simone, and you've just about attained the standard Simone had reached by the end of last year. But technique is only part of what makes a dancer, and what you lack in technique, you make up for in passion."

Hannah felt her spirits lifting.

"I'll admit I had some concerns at the start of the year," Miss Sabto continued. "At the end of Year Nine, you—or, should I say, Simone—left here a skilful, disciplined dancer, and you returned so different. But after your performance at the Dance Spectacular, your future here was never in question. There's a joyousness about your dancing, Hannah, that Simone never had. She was a perfectionist, but she never seemed happy, never had your animation." Miss Sabto paused, remembering her former pupil. "How is she doing?"

"She's fine," said Hannah.

"I'll need to confirm that," said Miss Sabto. "She's still officially enrolled in this school, and the VSD has a duty of care. I have to be sure that she's okay. In the meantime, we'd better go and tell Mr. Collins what you've just told me. Then we'll call your parents, and—"

"No!" cried Hannah.

"I beg your pardon?"

"No parents. Please," said Hannah, clearly distressed. "I'm just…not sure how they'll react."

Miss Sabto sighed. "We'll see the principal first and have a chat about how best to handle the situation. But I'm sure he'll agree they'll have to be told."

———

The break was over, and as Hannah and Miss Sabto left the classroom, a stream of students filed in. Hannah went to the bathroom to wash her face and drink some water, while Miss Sabto went in search of Mr. Collins. In the time it took to locate him, Hannah had a chance to think.

Now the three of them were sitting in the principal's office and Mr. Collins was listening to Hannah, open-mouthed.

"Unbelievable," he murmured when Hannah stopped speaking. He sat up straighter in his chair, then turned to Miss Sabto. "You had no idea she wasn't Simone?"

"None at all. At first I wondered why her technique wasn't as strong as it used to be, but then she showed such rapid improvement. And if her dancing lacked polish, it was certainly heartfelt."

"So you're pleased with her progress?" the principal asked.

"Absolutely. There was always a kind of tension in Simone's dancing, as if she were holding back. This year she seemed freer and more relaxed." Miss Sabto pulled a sheet of paper from a manila folder. "Here are some comments her teachers have written for the upcoming interviews. Jenny Hill: 'Simone is an accomplished jazz and hip-hop dancer with a vibrant and dynamic quality to her dancing.' Roderick Dixon: 'Simone is working well in both contemporary and pas-de-deux. She is a natural dancer with an exquisite line.' And we've talked about her in the staff room," Miss Sabto continued. "We all agree she dances with more abandon than she used to. And she seems happier, too. She—*Simone*—looked a bit miserable at the end of last year, though we had no idea she wanted to leave."

Hannah chewed her lip worriedly as Miss Sabto and the principal discussed her progress. Then Mr. Collins turned to face her.

"I've had a quick look at the progress reports for your academic subjects," he said. "Your marks in French are slightly lower than expected—though still above average. Other than that, you're doing fine."

Hannah twisted her hands in her lap. Now that Miss Sabto had acknowledged her potential, she burned with a renewed determination to keep her place at the VSD, no matter how unpopular she might be. "So...do you think I can stay?"

The principal tugged at his tie and nodded briefly. "When I talk to your parents, I'll recommend that you do." He paused, and, noting the concern on Hannah's face, continued kindly. "We can also strongly advise Ms. Stark that Simone should leave. We'll speak to your parents first, shall we?"

"No," said Hannah. "You can't. I mean, I don't want you speaking to my parents, or to Harriet. At least, not today. And not on the phone."

# forty-four

As the train sped toward the city, Simone glimpsed the unfamiliar suburbs rushing by. Since it was Sunday, there weren't many people on the train. The VSD, too, would be fairly deserted.

At the back of the carriage, a couple were kissing, and Simone recalled the precious afternoons she'd spent with Tom. A pang went through her. At least the next few Sunday afternoons would be taken care of—she'd be too busy to think of Tom.

The train pulled up at Flinders Street Station. Simone got off and walked toward the VSD. She couldn't wait to see Hannah—in fact, the best part about her sister's plan was the fact that they'd get to see each other every Sunday for the next few weeks.

It had taken all Hannah's powers of persuasion to convince Miss Sabto and the principal to go along with this idea. In the end, they'd agreed, though not without reservations.

Simone too had reservations, though for different reasons. Still, she wouldn't back out.

She wondered what it would be like to see Miss Sabto again. She'd always liked Miss Sabto—the ballet teacher had always been kind—but then, Simone had been a model pupil. Until this year, she'd never missed a single lesson unless she'd been sick or injured. Now she had in effect been playing truant for weeks. Under the circumstances, she couldn't help feeling a bit apprehensive.

Simone got off the train and rounded the corner to the VSD. Hannah was already at the entrance to the campus, and when the twins caught sight of each other, they ran toward each other, their faces wreathed in identical smiles. They wrapped their arms around each other and for a moment, all else was forgotten.

———

Apart from an initial, awkward moment, the reunion with Miss Sabto was surprisingly easy. "You look wonderful, Simone," the teacher said as she embraced her. "What have you been doing these last few months? Hannah's told me, of course, but I'd like to hear it from you."

As they crossed the courtyard, Simone spoke and Miss Sabto listened.

"Your new lifestyle must agree with you," Miss Sabto said when Simone had finished. "You really do seem well. You looked a bit peaky at the end of last year. I had no idea what you'd been going through."

"I know," said Simone.

"We staff do what we can to make sure our students are happy," the teacher continued, "but we're not mind readers. If you don't tell us you're having problems, we just can't know."

"No, of course not," said Simone. She thought of all the kids who starved themselves, or binged and then took laxatives, or threw up deliberately. The staff rarely knew—there was an unspoken pact to keep it a secret.

"Anyway," Miss Sabto continued, "are you okay with Hannah's plan?"

"Yes, I am."

"You don't think it's a bit...cheeky?"

"It is, a bit," Simone admitted. "But it's no worse than anything we've already done."

Miss Sabto gave Simone a wry smile. "You really are the spitting image of each other," she said, looking from Simone to Hannah and back again. "Still, I can't decide if what you did was very brave or very foolish..."

*Not brave*, thought Simone. Well, perhaps changing places with Hannah was a *little* brave, but it was mainly cowardly. She'd been so afraid of confrontation that she'd lacked the courage to face her own mother—to speak up for herself and make a stand.

She vowed that would change.

"Either way," Miss Sabto was saying, "I can appreciate why you acted as you did." She gave Simone another hug.

Simone felt a rush of affection for the compassionate teacher. Perhaps she could have confided in her all along.

Despite her faith in Miss Sabto, Simone became increasingly anxious as the end of term drew near. She still had no idea who'd sent those dreaded texts, and whether that person meant to expose them.

She and Hannah were so close to getting what they wanted—but everything depended on no one from home or school knowing the truth until she and Hannah were ready to tell them.

# forty-five

Hannah watched Harriet apply a second coat of lipstick and smooth down her hair.

"How do I look?" Harriet asked as she pulled on her jacket.

"Fine," said Hannah. "It's just a boring parent-teacher interview—it's not like you're going to the Oscars." Strange how Harriet was behaving as if she were the one who had to make a good impression.

In the car, while Harriet hummed along to the radio, Hannah sat quietly with her fingers crossed, hoping the evening would be uneventful. It was lucky that both Miss Sabto and Mr. Collins were such good sports and had agreed to keep her secret just a little longer. Even so, it would be all too easy for them to inadvertently give the game away.

Simone had warned Hannah that Harriet took the parent-teacher interviews *very* seriously. Still, Miss Sabto had promised to be diplomatic. Hannah would just have to trust her.

The car ride was over quickly. Harriet maneuvered the car into a tiny spot and turned to Hannah. "Right," she said. "Let's see what your teachers have to say."

―――――――――

The interviews were spread over five different classrooms, with three or four teachers assigned to each, their names on the door. With Hannah in tow, Harriet made a beeline for the classroom furthest from the main entrance, where she knew Miss Sabto would be waiting.

The teacher was deep in discussion with Julie and her parents, and two other students were already waiting.

"We could come back later," Hannah suggested. "Go see one of the other teachers in the meantime?"

"And miss our turn? No," said Harriet. "We'll see Miss Sabto first. Who's that girl talking to her? Is she in your class?"

Hannah nodded. "She's new this year."

"Is she any good?"

Hannah groaned. "Of course she is. That's why she got in."

"Don't make that face. I was only asking." Harriet tapped her foot as she waited first for Julie and then for the other two students to finish their consultation.

At last Miss Sabto called them over. She smiled at Harriet. "Ms. Stark," she said, "good to see you again."

Harriet gave a tight smile in return. "So," she asked, in a down-to-business tone of voice, "how is she doing?"

Miss Sabto glanced down at her notes, then up at Harriet. "How do *you* think she's doing?"

Harriet frowned. "I'm not the one who sees her in class. Why? Is something wrong?"

Miss Sabto quickly shook her head. "Simone is, as you know, a wonderful dancer..."

"But?"

"As talented as your daughter is," the teacher said, "I think I should warn you that dancing as a career is not for everyone. It's tough, emotionally and physically exhausting, and highly competitive."

"And you don't think she can handle it?"

"That's not what I said." Miss Sabto paused, choosing her words with care. "This school exists for two reasons," she continued. "One is to nurture talent. The other is to give our students options. All our students have potential, but only about one-third of them go on to become professional dancers, and we really don't mind, just as long as they're all happy and fulfilled." The teacher's tone was sympathetic but firm. "The goal of this school is not to produce dancers at any cost, but to empower our students."

"I'm not sure I understand you," Harriet said. "Are you saying that Simone lacks the drive to become a professional?"

"No, I'm saying she may not choose to make that commitment. *And that's okay.*"

"*Okay?* After all these years of training?"

"Yes," said Miss Sabto. "Education is never a waste. Ms. Stark, don't count on your daughter becoming a dancer—not because it isn't possible, but because it may not happen. We say this to all our students' parents. Your job, like ours, is to support them in their choices."

Harriet looked peeved and did not reply.

"Are you coming to next week's concert?" the teacher continued.

"Of course," said Harriet.

"Prepare yourself," said Miss Sabto, smiling. "You may be in for a surprise."

———————

It was dark by the time they left the school, and a tense silence filled the car.

"What an annoying parent-teacher interview," Harriet began. "Miss Sabto didn't say anything informative about your dancing, and I didn't like the implications of what she did say."

Hannah sat still in the passenger seat and didn't reply.

"There was something...not quite right about her," Harriet continued. "She was almost deliberately cagey." She braked sharply as the light turned red. "And what did she mean when she said I might be in for a surprise?"

Hannah said nothing.

"Simone? What surprise was she referring to?"

Harriet had turned to face her. Hannah looked her in the eye and aimed for a lightness of tone she hoped would mask her apprehension. "It wouldn't be a surprise if I told you, would it?"

The light turned green. Their car picked up speed as it crossed the intersection.

"There's something you're not telling me," Harriet said. "Something important, to do with school."

Hannah sighed. "Please, Mum, can we talk about it after the concert, over the holidays? It's only a week till the end of term."

# forty-six

As it turned out, Adam had been right to worry about the parent-teacher interviews. He'd been misbehaving in most of his classes, and while Simone sat reading in her room, the argument downstairs was becoming louder. The words "consequences" and "withdrawal of privileges" floated up the stairwell as Manfred and Vanessa remonstrated with their only son.

Later that evening, the defeated sound of his footsteps was followed by the creak of the door as he entered his bedroom. Would he let her console him? Having lived in fear of disappointing her mother, Simone knew how awful he must feel. And though he mightn't want her sympathy, she should at least offer some support.

The occasion seemed to call for silence, and she tiptoed quietly through the open door of Adam's room.

He didn't hear her as she came up behind him; he was too busy texting into his phone:

Wtch out! Ur secret ISNT safe with me!

Simone froze, disbelieving, as he pressed *send*.

In the next room, Hannah's phone beeped a moment later.

"Adam!"

He swung around, his face flushed with guilt.

"*You!*" she shouted, her face red with anger.

"What?" said Adam, his expression defiant.

She pulled him into Hannah's room, grabbed the phone, and showed him the message:

Wtch out! Ur secret ISNT safe with me!

"You did this," Simone said, her voice shaking. "You sent this text. You sent *all* those texts."

"What if I did?"

"I should throttle you," she yelled. "Do you know how much they freaked me out?"

Adam shrugged. "I wouldn't have even sent them if you'd just told me yourself. You never used to keep secrets from me."

"Get a life," she shouted. "And don't you dare—"

*Tell anyone*, she was about to say, when Adam interrupted with, "Relax, will you? I just wanted you to know I know."

Suddenly, it was as if he'd flicked a switch, and voice in her head said, *Hang on a minute*—what *does he know?*

Keeping her voice light, Simone asked calmly, "What is it that you think you know?"

"That you've got a boyfriend." Adam spoke in a childish, singsong tone.

Simone exhaled, only vaguely aware she'd been holding her breath. "What makes you think that?"

Adam paused before admitting, "I followed you...twice to Luna Park and the beach, and once to the botanical gardens."

"You *followed* me?"

"I was mad at you." Once again, a flash of guilt crossed his features.

"Mad at me, *why*?"

Adam shuffled his feet, avoiding her gaze. "You've been different ever since you got back from that summer dance course," he said at last.

Simone gulped air. "Different how?"

Now it was Adam's voice that shook. "You hardly ever share your music with me anymore, or grab the ball when I'm shooting goals. You never come bike riding with me, or hang out in my room. You...you've been ignoring me," he said. "It's like you don't care."

By the time he'd finished speaking, Simone's anger had subsided. A flush of shame crept over her cheeks.

"And I'm not the only one who's noticed," Adam continued. "I heard Mum and Dad talking about how you've changed."

Simone stiffened. "What did they say?"

Adam sniffed, then wiped his nose on his sleeve. "They think you're quieter and more withdrawn. But they're glad you're reading more and taking your schoolwork more seriously."

"They said that?"

"Yeah."

"In front of you?"

"Not exactly."

"So, you were eavesdropping?"

"No, I was standing outside their bedroom door."

The corners of Simone's mouth curled up in amusement. "What's so funny?" Adam said.

"Never mind. Look, I'm sorry I haven't hung out with you more. It's just that I've had a lot on my mind. But still," she said, her voice severe, "you had no right to spy on me."

"Sorry," said Adam, looking sheepish.

"And about that boyfriend you're so sure I have? He's not my boyfriend anymore. I haven't heard from him in weeks. Anyway, what makes you think I was keeping him secret?"

"He never hangs out with you and your friends."

"So?" Simone asked, folding her arms. "Why would I keep a boyfriend secret?"

"If he wasn't a secret, then why were you so freaked out when I threatened to tell?"

Simone narrowed her eyes. "I wasn't," she said, beginning to seethe.

"You just said you were."

Simone shook her head. "It wasn't the thought of people knowing I had a boyfriend that freaked me out—it was the idea of some psycho-stranger knowing something about me." She prodded his arm, none too gently. "There's such a thing as privacy, Adam. What you did was stalker-like and creepy. It was a really crappy thing to do."

"Sorry," said Adam, but Simone knew he wasn't entirely to blame. He'd wanted her company and she'd denied him. She'd been too self-absorbed to give him time, or find out what he was really like. She could only hope her oversight wouldn't effect his relationship with Hannah in the future.

"Apology accepted," said Simone, "as long as you never, ever do that again."

# forty-seven

The end-of-term concert at the VSD was underway. The Year Sevens, Eights, and Nines had already performed, and as the Year Nine dancers completed their final movements, the lights in the theater came on and Mr. Dixon walked onto the stage.

He coughed into the microphone and began: "Tonight, we're thrilled to bring you a very special performance." He was modulating his voice like a professional host, with just the right amount of tension and excitement. "Those of you who have been to our previous productions will no doubt remember the very accomplished Simone Stark, who has been with us since Year Seven."

An expectant hush came over the audience. Many leaned forward in their seats as Mr. Dixon continued: "Now, for the very first time..." The suspense in the theater was almost palpable—not a breath could be heard. "For the very first time, the lovely and very talented Simone will be dancing a duo with her equally lovely and talented"—here he paused for full effect—"*twin sister*, Hannah Segal."

While Mr. Dixon was speaking, Hannah and Simone stood in the darkened wings, watching their parents. Harriet's hand flew to her mouth, while beside her an astonished Manfred turned to Vanessa, whose dropped-jaw expression revealed her shock. Adam was perched on the edge of his seat, open-mouthed.

In the row behind them, eyes wide with disbelief, sat Sam, Liam, and—yes—even Tom, as well as Dani and some other girls from Carmel College.

"I've never been this nervous," Hannah said, clasping her sister's hand. "How about you, Sim? Are you okay?"

Simone took a deep and calming breath. "Yes," she said, and oddly, she was. This was the last time she'd ever have to dance onstage, and the knowledge freed her; her old anxiety just fell away. She would give it her all, because she didn't have to prove anything to anyone. Not anymore. "It's my final gift," she murmured softly.

"To who?" asked Hannah.

Simone glanced at her sister. "To myself, to you, and to my mother."

"Which mother?" Hannah whispered.

"All three of them," Simone said with a smile.

Onstage, Mr. Dixon was just completing his introduction. "Together, these two remarkable dancers will perform *Mirror Pirouette,* a unique and original work of art." As he spoke, the lights in the theater gradually dimmed. "And now, please welcome: Hannah and Simone."

There was a burst of applause, followed by a collective

gasp from the audience as the two identical girls stepped onto the stage.

Then the music began, the song chosen a rare version of "Man in the Mirror" sung by a female singer who belted out the lyrics and changed the word "man" to "gal."

The dance itself was a powerful mix of neoclassical and contemporary. The twins wore identical skin-colored bodysuits and, surprisingly, each girl wore only a single pointe shoe. Together the pointe shoes formed a pair, and when the two dancers stood in certain positions and at particular angles, they appeared to be one.

After building in intensity, the dance culminated in a series of *pirouettes*—Simone balancing on her right foot, Hannah on her left. At times the girls seemed to replace each other, define each other, become each other...

Their dancing was exactly matched, for Hannah's technique had improved beyond measure and Simone's dancing had lost some of its tension. With their pure energy and focus, they were simply mesmerizing, and as they lost themselves inside the dance, the audience too was lost, absorbed in the unfolding story.

As they spun, leapt, and flew across the stage, Simone's love of dance came flooding back, and she remembered what it was that had drawn her to it in the first place. She was grateful that her final performance was one of joy instead of heartache.

As for Hannah, she hoped her parents would see that this was just the beginning.

And now the dance was over and they were facing the audience, hand in hand, taking their bows. The audience was on its feet, whooping, whistling, demanding more. Simone and Hannah threw their arms around each other, then once again bowed to the audience, and the clapping and cheering continued even after they'd left the stage. Never before had either girl experienced such wild applause.

# forty-eight

Though the dance had been a huge success, the hardest part of the evening was still ahead. Back in the dressing room, the girls whipped off their costumes and removed their makeup. The time had come to face their parents.

Harriet was already standing in one corner of the green room, looking overwhelmed and dazed. Miss Sabto had gone to find Manfred and Vanessa and bring them backstage.

Simone took a deep breath and turned to Hannah. "Here goes," she said.

Hannah gave Simone a reassuring hug. "I'll come with you, if you like."

"No," said Simone. "I have to do this alone."

---

Simone walked across the green room carpet until she was standing in front of her mother. "Mum?"

"I think I'm in shock," Harriet said.

"I know. I would be, too."

"That performance was breathtaking. And Miss Sabto was right—it certainly was a huge surprise. How long have you known you had a twin?"

"Since Candance—that's where we met."

"Since *Candance*? But... why did you keep it a secret? When can I meet her?"

Simone held her mother's gaze. "You already have."

Harriet looked even more confused. "You mean...?"

"She's been living with you the entire term."

Harriet let out a tiny gasp. "Then where were *you*?"

"At Hannah's house."

"You went to live with total strangers?"

"Not strangers. Hannah's family."

Harriet stumbled, and Simone led her over to a chair and sat her down.

"You swapped places with Hannah? But why?" asked Harriet.

*Tell her. Just tell her,* thought Simone.

"I can't be a dancer," she explained. "And I couldn't face going back to the VSD, or home where I'd have to lie to you daily or else disappoint you." Tears pooled in her eyes, but Simone pressed on. "I've spent my whole life trying to be who you wanted me to be. I'm not sure you can understand this, but pretending to be Hannah was the only way I could really be me."

Harriet fought to regain her composure. "What does that mean, you can't be a dancer?"

"I just... can't," said Simone. "I always had such terrible

stage fright. I used to throw up before every performance, and I was so exhausted *all the time*."

Harriet was momentarily lost for words. Then she rallied. "We can fix that," she said. "There are ways to cope with stage fright. We can get you some counseling. Make sure you get the rest you need."

"No," said Simone, tears sliding down her cheeks. "I *won't* be a dancer."

"You wouldn't say that if you'd seen yourself onstage. You always look so composed and professional."

"It's a performance, Mum. It isn't real."

Harriet seemed not to have heard. "You're a wonderful dancer. And after all those years of training—"

"So I learned to dance," Simone said bravely. "Do you think that all kids who study math should become mathematicians?"

"No, of course not, but it's not the same."

"Yes, it is," Simone insisted. "I understand why you raised me to become a dancer. You did it out of respect for my birth mother, as a kind of tribute—you thought there'd be no one else to follow in her footsteps. But there is—there's Hannah. She *wants* to be a professional dancer."

"You could both be dancers," Harriet said.

"No!" Simone's voice was choked with frustration. "You're still not listening."

"I am, Simone. And I still say you can have a wonderful life and a brilliant career. That's all I want … all I've ever wanted for you."

"Why?" asked Simone, years of resentment surfacing. "Because it would reflect well on you?"

Harriet flinched. "That's not fair, Simone."

"Isn't it?" Simone's voice had risen in anguish. "I hate disappointing you," she said, "but I wish you could love me for who I am, not what I do."

"I do!" cried Harriet. "Of course I do."

A charged silence split the air as Harriet tried to come to grips with what Simone had said. "I do love you, Simone," she repeated. "I'm...very sorry you had to doubt it." Finally, she reached for her daughter and Simone let out a small sob as her mother embraced her. "I still can't believe you've been living with strangers."

"They're wonderful people." Simone sniffed and blew her nose. "They were sitting next to you, you know."

"Really, but how—"

"Hannah bought the tickets," Simone continued. "I told her parents and some of her friends that the VSD had invited selected students from other dance schools to perform, and that I—meaning Hannah—was one of them. They all believed me."

"Well, even I couldn't tell you apart...not in real life, and not onstage. That was an amazing performance, and you were both fantastic. You've obviously kept up your dancing..."

Simone nodded. "Three times a week. At Hannah's dance school. And Miss Sabto's been coaching us the last few Sunday afternoons. Ever since she learned the truth. It was Hannah's idea that we dance together—she wanted to show her parents what she could do."

Harriet frowned. "I'm shocked the school colluded with you."

"They almost didn't," said Simone. "They only found out three weeks ago. Hannah begged them not to tell you till the end of term."

"Hang on," said Harriet. "If you haven't been at the VSD, then where have you been going to school?"

"Carmel College. It's a really academic school, and I hope you'll let me stay there for now. It would be awful to change schools mid-year."

Harriet lifted a shaky hand to her head and smoothed down her hair.

"Mum, are you okay?"

Harriet sighed. "I suppose I am. It's just—it all seems so unbelievable. And finding out I haven't had *you* at home all this time... I feel as if I've been living a kind of lie."

"How do you think *I* felt when I first found out I had a twin?"

Harriet squeezed her daughter's hand. "I can only imagine. I wonder why the adoption agency never told us..."

"I bet Hannah's parents are wondering the same thing." As Simone spoke, the Segal family entered the green room. "Here they are now. They're coming to meet you."

# forty-nine

After Simone had entered the green room, Hannah went looking for her family. She was still fired up with adrenaline, still basking in the memory of that wild applause. What had her parents thought of the performance? It had been too dark in the audience to make out their faces when she and Simone had taken their bows, but surely they'd been bowled over by it. Surely they'd understand her now, and forgive her everything.

But what if, instead of seeing what a gifted dancer she was and how wonderful it was that she had a twin, all they could see was the deception?

It was a sobering thought, but when she found her parents outside with Miss Sabto, about to enter the stage door, she ran towards them. "Mum! Dad!" At the sound of her voice, Vanessa and Manfred turned toward her. "I've missed you so much," she said, flinging her arms around each in turn. "Wait, you do know that—"

"It's been months since we've seen you? Of course," said

Manfred. "I think we figured it out almost as soon as we saw you both onstage."

"And your teacher confirmed it," Vanessa agreed.

Hannah shot Miss Sabto a grateful smile.

"Now it makes sense," Vanessa was saying. "The pierced ears, the interest in reading, the switch to French ... And oh, that poor dentist!"

Despite her anguish, Hannah couldn't help but laugh.

"You and Simone might be genetically identical," Manfred continued where his wife left off, "but you're not entirely interchangeable. You're two different people."

"Then you're not angry?"

"We're your family, Hannah my love." Oh, it was wonderful to hear her father call her that. "The day we adopted you, we signed on to love you no matter what."

Tears sprang to Hannah's eyes and she blinked them away.

"So," said Vanessa gently, "what's it been like at the VSD?"

Hannah thought of all the ups and downs, the triumphs and the disappointments. Ultimately, it had all been worth it, and she knew without a doubt that despite the hardships and the challenges, this was where her future lay. "It's great to be in a place where dance is taken seriously. But I was pretty homesick," she admitted. "What did you think of that performance?"

"We could hardly believe our eyes when we saw the two of you onstage," Vanessa said. "That dance was magnificent."

"It was," Manfred agreed. "I only wish we could watch it again."

"You can," said Miss Sabto. "We thought the dance was so unique we've already filmed it and put it on YouTube—a bit of publicity for the school."

Vanessa put her arm around Hannah's shoulder and pulled her close. "I can't wait to watch that performance again. Maybe next time I'll be able to work out which dancer is you—though you were both superb. I was almost convinced you *could* become a professional dancer…"

"She could," said Miss Sabto, "if you let her stay at this school."

"So, can I?" begged Hannah. "Can I stay?"

Manfred and Vanessa exchanged a look. "Dance is a tough career path," Manfred began, "and there's no guarantee you'll even succeed."

"Dad's right," said Vanessa. "It's such a competitive field. And the slightest injury can end a career."

Hannah stood firm. "That's a risk I want to take."

Her parents exchanged another look, silently reaching an understanding.

"It's not what we'd have chosen for you…" Manfred said.

Hannah waited with bated breath, though a part of her knew they were about to yield.

"But if it's what you *really* want…"

"It is. It is."

"Then we'll help you achieve it."

For a second, Hannah was too choked up to speak. She hugged each parent in turn while Miss Sabto looked on, smiling broadly.

"It's getting chilly," said the teacher. "I think it's time we went inside."

"Right," said Hannah. "We should find Simone. By the way, where's Adam?"

"We left him chatting with Dani," said Vanessa. "You'll see him soon."

"I'll say goodbye now," said Miss Sabto. "It was lovely to meet you."

———

After Miss Sabto left, Hannah and her parents were about to enter the building when Hannah spotted Dani and Adam nearby. "Wait just a minute," she said to her parents.

"Hey, you two!" Without waiting to see how they'd react once they noticed her, or if they even knew which twin she was, Hannah threw her arms around each in turn. "If you only knew how much I've missed you—"

"That was an awesome performance, Hannah," Dani said, "but you don't deserve to be congratulated. Why didn't you confide in me? You were supposed to be my closest friend."

"I was. I am . . . "

"Then you've got a funny way of showing it." Dani glowered at Hannah, who looked at her pleadingly.

"You're not going to stay mad at me forever, are you? Dani, you can't!"

Dani shrugged, then relented. "I guess not," she said. Then, "Where's the bathroom? I need to pee."

Hannah pointed Dani in the right direction, then turned on Adam. "*You evil child!* Do you know how much you scared us with those nasty texts? I should wring your neck."

Adam looked sheepish under her gaze.

She gave his shoulders a little shake, then pulled him close.

"I was just pissed off," he mumbled, embarrassed.

"Well, maybe you had reason to be," Hannah admitted, her voice softening. "Simone told me what a lousy sister she was. I guess you just missed having *me* around. If it's any consolation, I missed you too." She hugged him again, making it clear that all was forgiven.

---

The intermission was over, and though the green room was now full of dancers ready to go onstage, Hannah had no trouble spotting Simone. "There she is. She's with her mum."

"Oh, the lady who was sitting next to us," Vanessa said.

Once the introductions were made, Manfred grabbed hold of Harriet, taking her breath away with one of his enormous hugs, and Simone looked on, unable to suppress a smile.

"Thank you," said Manfred. "Thank you for looking after our precious daughter."

Harriet composed herself enough to answer, "Thank *you* for looking after mine."

Then Simone stepped forward. "I'm sorry," she said to Hannah's parents, but they were already putting their arms around her, pulling her into their joint embrace.

"What for?" asked Manfred.

"You were both so wonderful to me, and I ... it was an imposition."

"No need to apologize," Vanessa said. "If I was in your shoes, I might have done the same.

"I'm sorry too," Hannah said to Harriet. "I know I gave you a really hard time."

Harriet nodded. "You did, at times," she said, giving Hannah an awkward pat, "but I realize now that it wasn't deliberate."

"Can ... can you understand why we changed places?" asked Simone, looking from Manfred to Vanessa.

"Of course," Manfred said. "Who wouldn't take the opportunity to walk in someone else's shoes?"

"Or in my case, dance in them," said Hannah.

Manfred chuckled. "Exactly. Even if you'd both had exactly the lives you wanted, I bet you'd still have swapped places—for the very same reason that people read. The closest most of us can get to someone else's life is through a book, but only identical twins can do it for real."

As soon as he mentioned the word "book," Hannah and Simone exchanged a smile, knowing he'd be unstoppable once he started on literature. Sure enough, he continued. "Stories of people swapping places are as old as the hills. There's *The Prince and the Pauper*, and the story of Jacob and Esau in the Bible. Who wouldn't change places—experience another life—if they had the chance? For identical twins, it's almost a birthright."

He wrapped his arms around both the girls. "Double the

beauty. Double the talent." He caught Harriet's eye. "Did you know your daughter was a twin?"

"No," said Harriet. "I was certain she was an only child. Although I did wonder why she came back from Candance almost a different person."

Vanessa smiled. "I know what you mean."

"If we'd known Hannah had a twin," said Manfred, "I'm sure we would have tried to adopt them both. In fact, I wonder ... could we be godparents to Simone?"

Hannah and Simone beamed at the prospect, and after a brief pause, Harriet nodded. "As long as I can be a godmother to Hannah, too."

# fifty

As the three parents talked, Hannah thought of all that had transpired since the dress rehearsal the previous morning, when the Year Ten dancers had finally found out the truth. She'd never forget how Jess, Mitch, and Matt had reacted—the shock on their faces—and how Matt had finally approached her and Simone.

He'd looked from one to the other. "Simone?" he'd asked.

"Yes?" said Simone.

"You never did go out with Tom, did you?"

"I did," Simone answered. "But I never went out with you. Before today, you hadn't seen me yet this year."

"So all this time," Matt said, turning to Hannah, "*you've* been pretending to be someone you're not?"

Hannah forced herself to meet his eye. "Yes," she admitted.

"I should have known," said Matt. "Simone was never interested in me before. And you... it was all an act. Why?

So that I'd help you with your dancing?" He sounded so hurt, so...betrayed.

"No," said Hannah, appalled he could think that. "Everything that happened between you and me—all that was real."

"Then why couldn't you trust me enough to tell me the truth?"

Simone had quietly moved away to give them some time alone.

"Simone and I promised each other we'd never risk it. But Matt," Hannah pleaded, "I was dying to tell you..."

Matt studied her face, trying to decide just what to believe.

"We couldn't take chances. The school didn't know!"

Matt seemed to have come to a decision, because suddenly his stance relaxed. "I've been pretty lousy to you these last few weeks, haven't I?" he said, his voice softening.

Hannah felt a ballooning of hope. "Yes, you have. So maybe we're even."

"I'm sorry, Sim—"

"Hannah," she said. "Hannah Segal."

Matt took a step closer. "I've missed you, Hannah Segal." And before she knew it he was kissing her, and it was almost like old times, only better, because she no longer had to hide the truth.

Later, when Mitch finally understood that Hannah hadn't betrayed Matt, and that Simone had only ever gone out with Tom, he'd agreed to phone Tom and persuade him to come to the performance.

"Tell him Simone wants him in the audience, but don't

tell him why," said Hannah. "That's for Simone to do. Tell him Sam and Liam will be there too."

True to their word, Sam and Liam had come to Melbourne for the Easter holidays. Hannah had bought tickets for all three of them, leaving them at the box office to be collected.

Now—with the performance behind them and their true identities revealed—Hannah and Simone slipped out of the greenroom to talk in private.

Hannah grinned at her sister. "We did it, Sim."

"I guess we did. But it isn't over. I still haven't seen Tom…"

For a moment, Hannah was quiet. "He's here, though," she said. "That's a good sign."

The second half of the performance was almost over. The two girls waited in the foyer of the theater, and when at last the audience came trooping out, they sought out their friends.

Since she was a head taller than anyone else, Sam was unmissable. On one side of her stood Liam. On the other stood Tom. He'd already seen them, but his face was unreadable, and Hannah wondered what he was thinking. "I'll go talk to Sam and Liam," she said to Simone. "You deal with Tom."

———

Here he was, not three meters away, with his dark, tousled hair and bottomless eyes. The pull Simone felt toward him was stronger than ever. He was looking right at her. What was he thinking? Would he ever forgive her?

They stared at each other across a space that was slowly filling with people.

And suddenly Tom was walking toward her.

A part of Simone wished she could run and hide, but she didn't move. By the time he reached her, her heart was pounding so loudly she was sure he could hear it.

For a second, Tom just stood and stared, his eyes roaming over her every feature. "Which one are you?"

The sound of his voice sent shivers down her spine. She longed to touch him. "Simone. I'm Simone."

"And at Candance?"

"It was me in class the very first morning. After that, it was Hannah. We'd met that lunchtime."

"How about the night at Koko Black?"

"That was me. It was Hannah who arranged the date."

"And when we got back to Melbourne?"

"Hannah arranged our meeting at Luna Park. But it was me who came."

"Sunday afternoons at the beach, and at the botanical gardens?"

"Me, all me."

Tom lowered his voice, as if afraid to hear the answer. "The Dance Spectacular?"

"I wasn't there."

"So you weren't the one who was kissing Matt?"

"No, that was Hannah."

Simone had the smallest sense that a weight was lifting…

"Tell me everything," said Tom.

Simone spoke, haltingly at first, and then more fluently. Now and again, Tom interjected, saying things like "Yeah, I wondered why you sounded so bossy that day on the phone," or "You were always so much sweeter when it was just the two of us."

When Simone paused for breath, Tom raked a hand through his thick, dark hair. "I just wish you'd told me the truth," he said.

"I wanted to," Simone admitted. "I came so close to telling you, but Hannah trusted me to keep it a secret..."

They'd left the theater and reached a bench in the courtyard. Simone perched on the wooden slats and Tom sat beside her.

"I was gutted when I thought it was you kissing that guy..."

"I'd never do that," said Simone.

"I know," said Tom. "I think I realized that when I saw you and your sister onstage. But I was mad at you for not being honest."

"And now?" asked Simone.

"I'm still trying to get over my injured pride, but I understand. You kept your sister's secret—that means you're trustworthy, and loyal too."

A slight breeze had started up, stirring Tom's well-remembered scent. It overpowered Simone's senses, almost making her forget that she hadn't actually apologized. "I'm sorry I caused you so much grief."

Tom turned an anxious face toward her. "I should be

the one apologizing. If I hadn't stormed off after the Dance Spectacular, Hannah might have explained."

Simone shrugged. "You were too upset to stay and listen."

"I guess it serves me right," he said. "These past few weeks have been … God, I've missed you."

"I've missed you too."

He put both arms around her, and she was so wrapped up in that one long, enchanted moment she forgot her name and who she was. It didn't seem to matter at all.

# fifty-one

Though the girls had made plans to spend one week of the holidays at Hannah's house and the other at Simone's, that night Hannah went home to Armadale and Simone went back to North Fitzroy. As Simone sat beside her mother in the car, they talked more openly and honestly than they had in years. And this time, Harriet listened.

"I'm sorry you had to spend so much money on my dancing—the leotards, the costumes, the expensive pointe shoes...I hope you're not angry."

Harriet sighed. "No, I'm not angry. At least, not at you. I should have known you were fed up with dancing. I should have seen the signs. And I shouldn't have pushed you into something you didn't want to do."

"You didn't know," said Simone. Now that she didn't have to return to the VSD, she could afford to be generous.

Harriet braked gently at a stop sign. "Do you want to keep dancing just as a hobby?"

"No," said Simone. "I've done enough dancing to last me a lifetime."

The car turned a corner, and Simone felt a rush of affection for the house she hadn't seen in months. It seemed smaller than she remembered, but warm and familiar.

Harriet led the way into the kitchen. "Do you have sugar in your tea?"

"No. Why?"

Harriet chuckled. "I guess it wouldn't matter if you did."

They drank their tea with the cheesecake Harriet had uncharacteristically stopped to buy.

"I was wondering," Simone said later, peering into the living room that looked more like a shrine to dance than a home, "do you think we could take down some of these photos?"

"Sure," said Harriet. "We can replace them with … whatever you like. Maybe some photos of you and Hannah and a few of your friends at Carmel College."

Simone smiled, relieved that she'd be allowed to stay at Hannah's school for the rest of the year, since Manfred had already paid the non-refundable annual fees.

"What about next year," Simone had asked, "and the year after that?"

Harriet said she couldn't afford a private school, but Manfred knew of several academically selective schools that offered full scholarships to deserving students. Given Simone's outstanding record, he was sure she'd receive one. Harriet agreed that Simone had earned the right to attend a school of her choosing.

"Thanks, Mum," Simone had said. "Thanks for being so understanding."

———————

The Segals' phone had not stopped ringing all day long, so quickly had the word spread. From close friends to mere acquaintances, suddenly everyone was interested in Hannah now that they knew she had a twin. By mid-afternoon, the dance on YouTube had already scored nearly a million hits, and phone calls were pouring in from the media with requests for interviews and information.

The most exciting phone call came from a filmmaker who wanted to make a documentary about the twins.

Hannah basked in the attention, which continued all week. As the weather grew cooler and the autumn air crisper, Good Friday ushered in a few quieter days. Passover and Easter coincided that year; the Segals were invited to the Starks' for an Easter egg hunt, and the Starks joined the Segals for the Passover Seder.

Then Hannah and Simone went on a double date with Matt and Tom. Now that both guys knew that neither was trying to steal the other's girlfriend, they were getting on fine.

"So, we got this phone call this morning," Hannah was saying, "from a producer who wants to make a documentary about us."

"Cool," said Matt.

But Tom was watching Simone with concern. "How do

you feel about it, considering you're not so keen on the lime-light?"

Simone was playing with his hand. "It's kind of exciting. I think our story is a good one, and good stories are meant to be shared. I said I'd do it as long as I don't have to dance again—I don't mind them using the footage from YouTube."

The four were crowded around a small table in Acland Street, and Matt's knee accidentally brushed Simone's when he pulled in his chair. At the sudden touch, she jerked away, pulling her chair closer to Tom's.

Matt rolled his eyes. "Jeez, Simone. I don't know how I thought that Hannah was you. You're just as uptight as you've always been."

"Watch it," said Hannah. "That's my sister you're insulting." But he'd said it good-naturedly, and they were all laughing.

Tom peered from one twin to the other. "You might look alike," he said, "but there's a different... energy about you. Now that I know there are two of you, I don't think I'd ever mix you up again."

# epilogue

**Three years later**

"*Mamãe, o que acontece?*" What happens next?

Marcela slipped the bookmark between the pages and placed the book on the bedside table. "You'll find out tomorrow." She planted a kiss on six-year-old Carlota's forehead and glanced at Mario. The four-year-old had nodded off.

Marcela settled back with her husband, Abilio, to watch *Fate or Coincidence?*, a documentary series that featured remarkable stories from around the world.

"Tonight," the host began, "we are delighted to bring you an extraordinary story of identical twins who found each other at the age of fifteen. Of special interest to our viewers in Brazil is the fact that they were born right here in Rio..."

Suddenly breathless, Marcela leaned forward and watched, enthralled, as two identical girls smiled into the camera. A shiver went through her.

"So, you started your lives in a Brazilian orphanage?"

The documentary was filmed in English, with Portuguese subtitles.

For a moment Marcela was back in that run-down orphanage, arguing with Beatriz. She'd often wondered what had become of the identical twin sisters. She wondered, too, what had happened to the sweet little girl she'd sent to Texas. She'd never spoken of her part in their futures to anyone except Abilio.

"Can you remember it? Can you tell us how you met?"

The girls described their meeting and their decision to swap identities.

"We have some footage of the performance where you danced together," the interviewer said.

Marcela had never seen anything quite so riveting.

Though both girls were exquisite dancers, only one had become a professional. The other saw her future in books, and had gone to university to major in English.

As Marcela continued to watch the sisters, small differences became apparent. The dancer was the more talkative of the two. The other seemed quieter and more reserved. Between them, they described the way their two families had become one, and the bond that grew stronger and stronger.

Marcela sniffed and blew her nose.

"Marcela, you're crying!" Abilio said. He put a comforting arm around her shoulder and pulled her close.

"They've found each other," Marcela said.

"I know, *meu querido*."

The documentary came to an end and the host was addressing the viewers at home. "We hope you enjoyed that remarkable story. As always, we leave you with just one question: *Fate or Coincidence?*"

Marcela smiled through her tears. Had nobody wondered whether Fate and Coincidence had both been given a helping hand?

## Acknowledgments

For editorial guidance, sincere thanks to Debbie Golvan, Yvonne Fein, Jane Godwin, and Brian Farrey-Latz. For unbridled enthusiasm, thanks to younger readers Avital Prawer and Rebecca Wein. For picking up on inconsistencies in an earlier draft, many thanks to Lital Weitzman. For thoroughness, dedication, and professionalism in assessing and reassessing each line of the novel, heartfelt thanks to Sandy Sullivan.

Thanks also to the friends and family who share my life and make it all worthwhile, and thank you, readers, for allowing my writing into your lives.